INVASION

BOOK ONE OF THE PROTECTORATE

Jeffrey Harlan

Confluent Press™

Thank you to my family and friends for your support and encouragement, especially to my wife, Megan, and the NOC Writing Community on Discord.

CHAPTER ONE

John Chambers tugged at the collar of the costume—the *uniform,* he reminded himself—as he waited behind the curtain. John was young, having only recently turned eighteen years old, and he had already been thrust into a position of authority that he wasn't sure that he was ready for.

John had super powers. Until now, that had meant that he would more than likely be drafted into the military. He could have gotten a deferment on that, as he had already been accepted to the University of Nevada, Las Vegas, but four years of mandatory military service was all but inevitable for anyone with a tactically valuable super power, and combat seemed extremely likely if he was drafted.

Superhumans had been around since the 1950s, when Nucleus and Strongman first came out as superheroes. It took time, but the world adjusted. For about a decade, it started to look like superheroes would become the new normal, at least in the United States, but that all changed in 1962, after the Cuban Missile Crisis.

Congress passed the Superhuman Induction Act after that, drafting everyone with super powers. It was—and remained—a highly contested piece of legislation. It briefly went away during the Carter Administration, but the Soviet invasion of Afghanistan in 1980 led Congress to bring it back again after only three years. The SIA remained largely unchanged until 1993, when President Clinton pushed legislation to amend the law so that superhumans only had to register, as with the

Selective Service Act, and exceptions were added for anyone pursuing a career in public service, such as police or emergency services, or a civilian position with federal, state, or local government.

The SIA's draft provisions came back in full force again after the terrorist attacks on September 11, 2001. Within a week, President Bush signed legislation that reinstated the superhuman draft, and fifteen years later, it was still the law. President Obama had vowed to repeal it during his re-election campaign in 2012, but a Republican majority in Congress had blocked him from fulfilling that campaign promise. Now it was 2016, Obama was in his final year as president, and nothing had changed. Hillary Clinton was running for the presidency, and had made a similar promise, but few believed it would actually come to pass.

But loopholes existed, thanks to a patchwork of amendments to the SIA over the decades. Exceptions were allowed. A few states had followed New York's lead, allowing teams of superhumans to be licensed as private security, deputized police, or even as state militia forces. Slowly, superheroes were returning, after a fashion. John's father ran an incredibly successful corporation, and his legal team had found the opportunity to create such a team around John, which would shield him and the other team members from the SIA's military draft.

And that's how John found himself as the leader of a team of superheroes at eighteen years old. He didn't want to be drafted, and his father made it happen. He didn't know how to feel about that.

As part of his new role, John had been tapped to conduct the interviews for potential members of the team. The process had been, largely, boring and repetitive, with only a few individuals he'd met with who stood out. Most of the applicants had been rejected fairly quickly; their powers were often useless for a team focused on superhuman emergency response. Some didn't even have the powers they'd claimed, and had only come seeking attention. Most of those had, at least, been weeded out in the selection process before they got to him.

Of those that didn't make the team but were nevertheless memorable, the top of the list had to be the one who called himself Leafmaster. He was a few years older than John; his application said that he was a student at UCLA. He showed up wearing a homemade costume: a light green spandex outfit with a dark green cape, boots, and trunks, and an enormous dark green leaf on his chest. The costume did him no favors, both physically and in terms of the initial impression it left John with. He remembered the incident vividly.

— § —

"Call me Leafmaster!" the young man exclaimed eagerly as he stood opposite the desk where John, in jeans and a cream-colored dress shirt, sat, slack-jawed. Putting his fists on his hips, Leafmaster stood in an overly-dramatic pose.

"Uh," John began uncertainly, the weirdness of the encounter throwing him off-balance, "okay, mister..." John trailed off, trying to retain his composure. He tried again, "Mr. Leafmaster. What—"

"What can I do?" the dark-skinned man asked, finishing John's question. He grinned, pushing his glasses up on his nose before reaching into a bag by his feet. He pulled out a potted plant, and set it on the table in front of John. "I make plants grow!" he exclaimed in excitement. "Any plant!"

Indeed, the plant in question, a small, white flower, began to grow vines. They spread out from the flower pot at an impressive rate, covering the table in moments, the vines undulating like tentacles.

"That's," John began, trying to choose his words diplomatically, before deciding on, "*different.*"

Leafmaster seemed oblivious to John's hesitation. "Imagine!" he continued in his excitement, spreading his hands as though giving a presentation for his college professors. "Giant venus flytraps to capture—"

"Yeah," John interrupted. He'd seen enough. Making plants grow? There was no way that could be tactically viable. "That would be great, if we were in *Wisconsin.*" Even in the moment, John wondered why he'd picked that particular state as an example. It was a more temperate climate, and he had family there on his mom's side, so that was probably the reason why. "But this is Vegas. A desert." Leafmaster looked crestfallen. John sympathized, but he wasn't what the team needed. "Sorry," John added, hoping to soften the blow. Leafmaster stood there, blinking in disbelief. John waited for several seconds, his patience drawing thin, before finally calling, "Next!"

Leafmaster finally grabbed his bag, then left the room. As he left, the vines on the table, having now wrapped completely around the middle, flexed… and the table snapped in half. *Was that just from the weight of the plant,* John wondered, *or did Leafmaster do that?* He sighed. His decision had been made, and the would-be superhero was already gone.

John held his head in his hands, his elbows resting on his knees, as the next candidate entered the room. Looking up, he saw a tall, thin young man with light skin and dark brown hair standing before him on the other side of the broken table, wearing jeans and a green t-shirt.

Returning from his reverie, John looked at the people around him. That man in the green shirt was now standing behind John. There were six of them in all, wearing nearly-identical uniforms. The uniforms were made from a lightweight, bulletproof fabric first developed decades earlier by a superhero known as the Wizard. Sales of the material to other superheroes and to the government had made him a fortune. The uniforms were reminiscent of biker leathers in their design, if not their material, with a black jacket and pants that tucked into padded, combat-style boots. The arms and shoulders, and the sides of the pants legs and the boots' padding all featured brightly-colored fabrics, which were unique to each of the wearers.

John's uniform featured bright red fabric and yellow piping, reflecting his powers: John had the ability to generate and control fire, known as pyrokinesis, as well as the ability to fly, which had earned him the superhero name Pyre.

To his right was Danielle Thompson, a friend of John's—Pyre's—from school. She had been dubbed Psyche, due to her telepathic and telekinetic abilities, and her uniform featured green fabric with yellow piping. She was a petite young woman, with brown hair that she kept in a shoulder-length bob.

To Pyre's left was another friend of his from school, Kevin Burke. Kevin had the ability to create forcefields in geometric shapes, earning him the name Sphere. His uniform complemented his bright red hair with orange fabric and yellow piping.

Behind Danielle—Psyche when in costume, Pyre reminded himself—was Jim Williamson. He had olive skin, which he had inherited from his mother, and his hair was a shade of brown slightly darker than his skin, a trait which had come from his father's side. His shapeshifting powers, virtually unheard of in the superhuman community, were formidable, and had earned for him the name Versipellis, taken from a Latin word that meant "changing skins." His powers meant that, rather than wearing a uniform like the others, he *became* the uniform, shifting part of his body to resemble whatever clothing he wished. He had chosen purple fabric with orange piping for his colors.

Behind Sphere stood the only other female member of the team, a dark-haired Latina named Nicole Harris. She wore red fabric like Pyre, but with light blue piping instead. She had the ability to generate electricity, almost like an electric eel, but at far stronger levels, and she had been dubbed Singe.

Rounding out the team, David Brown stood behind Pyre. During his interview, Pyre discovered that David was the grandson of the first superhero, Nucleus, and had inherited his ability to generate plasma, which could be used both as a weapon as well as to fly. Taking his grandfather's heroic identity as his own, the new Nucleus' uniform had yellow fabric with blue piping, echoing the colors of the first Nucleus' own costume.

The curtain parted as a voice called out from the other side off the stage, "Ladies and gentlemen, without further ado, I give you Las Vegas' first superhero team: the Protectorate!" Lights blazed onto the stage, making it difficult to see the crowd beyond, but Pyre knew that dozens, if not hundreds, of people were seated in the audience for the team's debut and press conference. A roar of applause greeted them, and the camera flashes broke through from beyond the glare.

Pyre and the rest of his team stepped forward, spreading out to line up together on stage for the photographers. He looked to the podium as the speaker continued to introduce them.

The speaker was Pyre's father, Max Chambers, the founder and CEO of Chambers International, and corporate backer of the Protectorate. Pyre looked very much like a younger, more athletic version of his father, albeit with blond hair and no need for eyeglasses. Max Chambers had started his company here in his hometown of Las Vegas, and its meteoric rise to become an international conglomerate was all but unprecedented, save for the likes of contemporaries like Amazon and

Google. Max had an uncanny ability to pick winning moves, so even when markets dropped, Max still managed to stay ahead.

Some speculated that Max must have some form of precognition or clairvoyance, based on his incredible business acumen, but he denied having abilities of any kind. The rumors persisted, of course, but Pyre doubted his father had anything more than a keen business sense. If he truly had been clairvoyant, Pyre reasoned, then surely he would have been able to foresee and prevent his divorce from Pyre's mother... wouldn't he?

And if he had been clairvoyant, he also would have foreseen the man in the olive drab t-shirt and jeans storm into the auditorium at the Chambers Casino and Resort. The man with dark, mocha-colored skin and shaved, dark brown hair. The man with an infuriated scowl and glowing fists. He shoved past the security guards, knocking them over easily as he stormed into the room. He rose his right arm, pointing toward the stage. *Aiming.*

They weren't ready for this. They had barely begun to get to know one another, let alone train together to fight against bad guys. Trained or not, the moment was here.

"Sphere, shield!" Pyre yelled as the blast of plasma ripped from the man's fist toward the stage. It impacted harmlessly against the hastily-erected forcefield, protecting Pyre's...

Wait, Pyre thought. *My dad* wasn't *the target.*

The plasma had hit just to Pyre's left, while his father was on the end of the stage to his right. He looked to his left, and saw Nucleus. The young legacy hero didn't look surprised, or angry, or even scared. If anything, he looked *disappointed.*

"Jesus Christ," he muttered. "*Really?*"

Pyre, Versipellis, and Singe leaped off the stage and rushed the man, who fired another blast of plasma the moment he realized that Sphere's forcefield had dropped. It struck Nucleus in the chest, sending him flying backward, and Sphere moved to help his teammate while Psyche escorted Max off the stage and to safety. The crowd fled the room, rushing the exits, but a handful of fearless photographers and reporters were holding back, trying to get the story that was unfolding before them.

Psyche returned to the stage as Nucleus sat up, and she and Sphere helped him to his feet. Looking out toward the overturned tables and chairs in front of the stage, they could see Pyre, Versipellis, and Singe attempting to subdue their intruder.

Versipellis was shifting his upper body into his preferred combat form: a chitinous red, segmented body armor not dissimilar from an insect's exoskeleton, with his fingers becoming sharp talons. His lower body liquefied and stretched, and he began to wrap himself around the intruder.

Singe ran up in front of the man, electricity crackling from her fists much like the plasma that roiled around his so intently that the bones in his hands were visible through his skin. Pyre hovered in midair behind the man, flames engulfing his hands.

"Give it up, buddy," Pyre said. "Whatever your problem is, this isn't the way."

The intruder unleashed a wave of plasma that pushed Pyre, Versipellis, and Singe back, knocking them all over. He assumed a crouched fighting stance, his right fist clenched and held near his chest, his left held ready to strike from behind his back.

"'Buddy?'" he repeated angrily. "My name's not 'buddy!' It's Plasmid! My goddamn name is *Plasmid!*"

"Geez, Nucleus," Sphere said, standing at the edge of the stage with his teammate. "Dude's got the same powers as you!"

"Not surprising, really," Nucleus said, rubbing the back of his head, which he'd hit on the stage floor when Plasmid's second attack sent him flying. "He *is* my brother, after all."

Chapter Two

"Half-brother!" Plasmid shouted almost immediately. *"Half-brother, you son of a—"*

"Don," Nucleus interrupted forcefully, pointing a finger at his sibling, "have some respect for mom."

"Go to hell!" Plasmid retorted angrily, the plasma around his fists surging brighter. He glared at Nucleus and yelled, "You don't know what it's like to suffer! You don't know pain! *None* of you do!" Singe and Versipellis both recoiled at Plasmid's words. For them, at least, they couldn't have been further from the truth.

Singe—Nicole Harris—grew up suffering at the hands of an abusive stepfather. Her mother and he were both abusive, particularly when they were drunk, but he was the worst of the two. She was twelve years old when her stepfather began abusing her with more than his fists.

She became increasingly uncomfortable and scared with the way that he had begun touching and holding her, and when she finally gathered the courage to say so, he exploded with rage.

Spewing obscenities, he threw her to the floor. Nicole cowered as he told her that her mother wasn't home, and that she was going to be at work all night.

He stalked toward her, his white tank top stained with cheap beer. His fists were clenched, ready to "teach her a lesson." He grabbed her by one of the pigtails that she liked to wear her hair in. His breath reeked of cheap alcohol, and Nicole turned her head away as he tried to kiss her mouth. He slapped her, hard, across her face.

Tears streaming down her cheeks, Nicole tried to move away from him again, and found herself literally backed into a corner. The lime green wallpaper was peeling, revealing layers of older wall coverings beneath. He grabbed at her shirt, trying to lift it and remove it. She put her hands up, trying to push him away, but he was too big, too strong. She wanted him off of her, but he wouldn't stop. She closed her eyes, turning her head again as he clumsily tried to kiss her once more. She pushed as hard as she could.

And suddenly, he wasn't on top of her anymore. After a moment, Nicole dared to open her eyes again. Sparks crackled between her fingers, her arms still held straight out in front of her. A few feet away, her stepfather lay on his back, his eyes wide and not blinking, his mouth slightly open as though surprised. Thin wisps of smoke rose from small, blackened handprints left on his shirt, on each side of his chest. Nicole sat up, wrapping her arms around her legs. She buried her face in her knees and began to cry.

Versipellis—Jim Williamson—also had endured his own pain as a child, though of a different sort than Singe. When he was eight years old, he lived with his mother and father in Los Angeles. His parents were devoted, caring, people who worked hard to provide for their son.

Jim was walking outside with his father after school. He'd done well on a test and his dad had promised to take him out for ice cream. They were making their way to the parking lot near their apartment complex, and were walking on the sidewalk near a relatively busy street while Jim was telling his dad all about what he'd learned in school that day. He was in the middle of recounting a story he'd heard in class about the Native American tribes that had lived in the area before the Spanish settled and began to build their missions when tires screeched and a car's engine roared behind them.

Jim started to turn around to see what the commotion was about when his dad grabbed him by the shoulders. His dad pulled him hard, spinning around with his back to the street as gunfire roared through the neighborhood. As the car drove past, Jim saw several people with guns hanging out of the windows, firing wildly and yelling incoherently. Seconds later, the car sped away.

Jim's father fell over on top of him, then onto the sidewalk. Jim knelt down next to him, and he could hear that his father was having trouble breathing. His white shirt was turning red as blood pooled on the ground underneath him and seeped out of a large hole near his shoulder. His father groaned through clenched teeth and his face contorted in pain.

"Are you all right?" he managed to gasp out. "Please be okay."

"I'm okay," Jim said, trying to hold back tears. He was scared. His dad had always been so big and strong, and now he was hurt and bleeding. His father reached up and put a hand on his cheek, wiping away tears. Then his hand fell, limply, back down to the ground.

Jim saw that his father's eyes were closed. He looked like he was sleeping, but not. He tried to wake his father, but he didn't respond. He shook his shoulders, but he wouldn't wake up. Jim started to cry uncontrollably. As he cried, his hands began to change. They became a hard, red, chitinous shell with razor-like fingers.

Singe surged toward Plasmid, whose attention was now focused on Nucleus. Electricity crackled madly around her fists, and Versipellis quickly wrapped himself around her, restraining her.

"You don't know what the hell you're talking about!" Singe spat at Plasmid.

"Easy, Nicole!" Versipellis said, having wrapped himself around her waist and arms. "He's not worth it!"

Pyre stepped toward Plasmid, more calmly now that the situation was less volatile than it had been just a couple of minutes earlier. Plasmid still had a roiling cloud of plasma surrounding his energized fists, and Pyre kept his right hand aflame as he pointed with his now-extinguished left hand at Plasmid.

"Why are you attacking us?" Pyre demanded.

"I don't give a damn about you," Plasmid retorted. "I'm after David!"

Nucleus hopped down from the stage to speak to his enraged sibling. "But... why?" he asked, confused.

"Why?" Plasmid repeated angrily. "*Why?*" He pointed an accusing finger at Nucleus, but had finally dissipated the plasma surrounding his fists. "Your dad gave you everything! You went to college! I couldn't afford tuition and got drafted 'cause I'm a freak!" Plasmid's anger was renewed at the memories, and his hands remained balled up into fists.

Their mother had divorced Nucleus' father and, less than a year later, was remarried to Plasmid's father. The divorce had been contentious, and Nucleus—David—had stayed with his father in the end. Six months after she had remarried, Plasmid—Don—was born. The two boys had little contact with one another as they grew up. David and his father remained in Las Vegas, while Don grew up in Southern California. Don grew up acutely aware that his older half-brother always lived better than he did: better clothes, better school, and better opportunities all around, and his bitterness only grew as he got older.

David was just over two years older than Don, and had spent those last two years as a student at UNLV. His status as a college student had exempted him from being drafted, another circumstance unavailable to Don. Less than a year ago, after turning eighteen, he had been drafted into the Marine Corps. Despite his abilities, which Don was certain should have earned him an immediate posting to Team Liberty, the military's elite joint-service team of superhuman soldiers, he was instead shuffled to what he felt was a dead-end posting at Camp Pendleton, less than two hours' drive from where he had grown up.

The final straw was when he had learned that David was going to become a superhero like their grandfather, and that he would be permanently exempted from the draft as a result. Something inside of him had snapped, and Don—now going by the code name Plasmid, which he'd been given while in the military—came to Las Vegas to confront his sibling.

Nucleus was dumbstruck for a moment, but found his words again after a moment. "You think," he began incredulously, "my dad paid for my education? Hell, no! *I* did!" He pointed to himself with his thumb for emphasis.

"But I," Plasmid began, his confusion clearly evident. "I mean you—" He stopped again. "How did you—"

Nucleus slapped his forehead with the gloved palm of his hand. He rolled his head back, a pained expression on his face. "Scholarships, genius," he finally said after a moment. "Grants. Loans. Part-time jobs. Whatever it took!"

Before the conversation could continue any further, a trio of armed men in camouflage uniforms burst through the doors. They wore black berets with a black armband attached to the right shoulder of their uniform; on the armband, in large white letters, it read "SP," and the left pocket of their uniform bore an embroidered patch in the shape of a police badge below the "U.S. Air Force" patch. The man in the middle of the trio of military policemen was a large Black man with "Hare" embroidered on the nametape above his uniform shirt's right pocket, and the four stripes of a staff sergeant on his sleeves. The two others standing immediately behind and to either side of Sergeant Hare, a thin white man with sandy hair and an Asian man, both with the three stripes denoting the rank of Senior Airman, had their sidearms drawn and held in a ready position.

Pointing his 9mm Beretta semiautomatic pistol directly toward Plasmid, Sergeant Hare called out, "Nobody move!" He steadied his aim, then continued, "Private First Class Donald Bryton, you are under arrest!"

Nucleus glanced at Plasmid and said, "You went AWOL, didn't you?" He sighed, briefly closing his eyes and shaking his head, then muttered, "Jesus, Don."

Sergeant Hare cautiously advanced toward Plasmid, who had his hands held up in a universal gesture of surrender. As he approached, he continued speaking, never lowering his aim with his firearm. "You are charged with dereliction of duty," Sergeant Hare said, "striking a superior officer, assault with a deadly weapon, and absence from your place of duty without authorization."

As the other two Security Forces airmen took their positions in support of Sergeant Hare, aiming their pistols at Plasmid as well, Hare returned his pistol to its holster at his waist, then retrieved a pair of handcuffs. Never taking his gaze from Plasmid's eyes until he stepped behind the young superhuman, he grabbed Plasmid's left arm by the wrist and yanked it downward. He snapped one end of his handcuffs around Plasmid's wrist, and asked, "Do you understand these charges, Marine?" He grabbed Plasmid's other wrist, then secured it with the handcuffs behind Plasmid's back as well.

As Sergeant Hare reached into a pouch on his belt to retrieve something, Plasmid replied, "Yes, Staff Sergeant." Hare lifted a small item, which he held between his thumb and two fingers, to Plasmid's face, just under his nose, and squeezed. There was a slight snapping sound as glass broke within the cloth container, and Hare held the item in place under Plasmid's nose for a few seconds.

Sphere recoiled, taking a step backward from where he still stood at the edge of the stage. "Jesus Christ!" he exclaimed, holding his hands up defensively in front of himself, his eyes wide in horror.

"Is that what I think that is?" Versipellis asked, a worried look on his face as well.

Sergeant Hare held the small piece of cloth up, where the others could see it more easily. It was bent in the middle, where a glass ampule within had been broken, and the cloth was now damp. "Dampening gas," Hare confirmed, "yes."

Nucleus took a step back as well, and ignited a cloud of plasma around his own fist. "It's nerve gas!" he exclaimed.

"Non-lethal," Sergeant Hare explained, stowing the used ampule in a pouch on his belt, "and the effects are temporary. Especially at such a low dose."

"That's not the point," Pyre said, pointing a finger at Sergeant Hare.

"What do you care?" Hare asked, incredulously. "He attacked you!"

"He's my brother!" Nucleus replied, pointing at Plasmid. Instantly, Hare better understood the situation.

"Look," he said, holding up a hand in hopes of calming the young heroes' nerves and reassuring them, "dampening gas is standard procedure, for our safety as much as his. It temporarily paralyzes the part of the brain that controls his powers. It'll wear off in a few hours, and the worst he'll get is a headache and a runny nose."

The Security Forces airmen escorted the handcuffed and temporarily de-powered Plasmid out of the room, where their police cars presumably waited outside. Sergeant Hare followed, then stopped as he reached the exit. Holding the door as he stood at the exit, he turned and looked back toward Nucleus. "Have a good day, sir," he said, then exited as well.

Nucleus fumed in frustration and anger. "Damn it," he muttered as he noticed that the reporters and photographers were still there, recording the entire sordid encounter for posterity.

Chapter Three

Several days passed without any further incidents, following the brief but memorable press conference. In the hallways of Arbol Verde High School, on the western edge of Las Vegas, John Chambers leaned against the row of lockers as his friend, Kevin Burke, rummaged through his open locker. Kevin scowled as he grabbed one of the textbooks he had stacked within, then shoved it angrily into his backpack.

Students packed the hallway as they made their way from one class to another. They jostled one another, a mass of young humanity scurrying from one location to the next, books in hand, bags slung across their backs. Some laughed with their friends, some silently tried to keep to themselves as much as they could in a crowded hallway.

Kevin slammed another book into his backpack, and John looked at his friend with concern. "Everything all right?" John asked, stepping away from the lockers that he'd been leaning against to face his friend more directly.

"Oh, just peachy," Kevin replied, his tone thick with sarcasm. "Why would you think otherwise?"

"Well," John said, "you seem pissed off. Anything I can do to help?"

Kevin laughed bitterly, pausing from his task momentarily. He turned his head to look at John. "Not unless you can get me back on the football team," he said. "You know how this school is about sports."

As Kevin reached inside of his locker for another textbook, John adjusted his backpack and tried to cheer his friend up. "C'mon, Kevin," he chided lightly, putting his best smile on for his friend, "admit it: being a super hero is cooler than being on the football team."

"Is it, John?" Kevin asked, zipping up his bag. He slung the bag over his shoulders and shut his locker before continuing, "I got retroactively kicked off the team because of my powers. I never cheated, but some people won't believe that."

The full truth was, of course, somewhat more complicated than that. Superhumans were barred from competing in organized sports, as parents' groups had pushed for decades earlier, because of the perceived unfair advantage that one team could have over another, should players use super powers that their competitors did not possess. Super speed, telekinesis, super strength, teleportation... all of these could be misused by a student athlete, intentionally or otherwise. To keep the playing field even, rules had been created that, at least at the high school and collegiate levels, kept superhuman students from competing in organized sports. Thus far, no one had managed to successfully challenge those rules.

John and Kevin started walking away from the locker. They were so intent on their conversation, they didn't realize the crowd had begun to thin considerably around them. "Who cares?" John asked. "I believe you. All of your friends believe you, and we're here for you!"

"John," Kevin said, his voice mixed with anger, frustration, and sadness as he stopped and turned to face his friend, "we had to forfeit every game I played in! We were undefeated!" He shook his head, trying to will away the frustration, and lowered his voice nearly to a whisper. "Everyone hates me now."

"Not everyone," a voice said from behind them in the all-but-empty hallway. They turned and saw Danielle Thompson, now becoming more publicly known as Psyche, standing in the hallway, her backpack by her side in her left hand. She stepped between John and Kevin, looking at Kevin as she continued, "Yes, people are angry, but not at you." She paused a moment, then clarified, "Not most of them."

"And who'd know better than a telepath, right?" Kevin asked, adjusting the straps on his backpack.

"Damn straight," Danielle replied. She threw her arms over the shoulders of her friends. "C'mon," she said, "let's get moving. I don't want to have to make everyone think we're on time for English again!"

—§—

Later that evening, Jim Williamson and Nicole Harris stood side-by-side at an arcade game cabinet at a video game arcade located just off the Las Vegas Strip. The place was enormous, and held hundreds of arcade cabinets; some were classic arcade games dating back decades, while some were newer. Hundreds of people—mostly teenagers and young adults, but also a few older adults looking to relive part of their childhoods with the classic arcade experience—milled about the large, multi-level arcade facility. Music, game sounds, and a cacophony of voices filled the air around them.

Jim and Nicole deftly moved the joysticks and rapidly smashed the buttons on the machine. On the screen, animated figures leaped, punched, kicked, and blocked one another, the image of a devastated city street in the background. The sounds of video game fighters grunting, punching, kicking, and yelling accompanied their movements, and was underscored by a pulsing beat of techno music. The health bar at the top corner of the screen next to Nicole's fighter continued to dwindle, and she bit her lip in concentration. Something caught her attention out of the corner of her eye, just below the screen: something had moved and it didn't look right.

"Hey!" Nicole said indignantly, yet playfully. "No fair! Lose the extra digits, Jim!"

Caught, Jim pulled the extra fingers that he'd grown on his right hand back into his hand. Grinning despite everything, he kept playing the game without comment. Restricted to a normal number of fingers, his character's attacks and special moves came less frequently, and Nicole began to return the damage inflicted upon her character onto Jim's. The game lasted several more minutes, but the final blow ultimately came, and Nicole's character stood victorious, one foot mounted atop the fallen body of Jim's character. The animated fighter raised her fists in the air in triumph, and let loose a victory cry. Nicole turned her head to look at Jim, and playfully stuck out her tongue.

"Let's get some dinner," Jim suggested. The two had met just a few weeks earlier, when they came together for the first team meeting for the Protectorate. They had taken an instant liking to one another, and had started dating not long after. Though the circumstances of their childhoods were quite different, they bonded over shared trauma, as well as a feeling of "otherness" compared to the other members of the team, particularly Pyre, Sphere, and Psyche, who were already old friends from their high school.

Jim attended a different school, as he lived in a far less affluent part of town. After his father's death during that drive-by shooting in Los Angeles, Jim's mother eventually found a job in Las Vegas, as a housekeeper at one of the casino resorts. The pay was not great, but the cost of living in Nevada was better than that in California, and they moved. Even now, nearly a decade later, they still struggled to make ends meet, and Jim answered the call to try out for the team more to help his mother financially and to be able to stay nearby, rather than face being drafted into the military and sent who-knows-where by the U.S. government.

Nicole had lived an equally difficult life after the death of her stepfather when her powers first emerged. She had been placed into the foster care system when the investigation revealed how she had been mistreated by both her parents, and how her own mother had been willing to look the other way and ignore the abuse she was suffering from her stepfather. She had lived with several different families, some of whom had been genuinely interested in helping her, while others had only taken in foster children for the money they received from the state.

Too often, she had come home from school to find her meager belongings stuffed into a garbage bag, and was told that she was going somewhere else. Sometimes that was another family's home. Sometimes that was a state-run home for foster children. Those times were even worse; she fought with the other children, many of whom tried to steal what few belongings she owned. Some of the boys there tried to pressure her into sex, which typically earned them a jolt of electricity in a sensitive area. She hated every moment of it, and was glad when she finally turned eighteen and finished high school.

She had no desire to go into the military, and had enrolled at the Community College of Southern Nevada. Attending college was a short-term solution to avoid the inevitable military draft, but it was the only thing she could do. She had hoped that something would happen, from the long-promised repeal of the Superhuman Induction Act to some other unforeseen eventuality that would prevent her having to enter the military, in the time that it took her to complete a degree, but she knew deep down that it was really just avoiding the inevitable.

Then the call came out for superhumans to try out for the Protectorate. She tried out right away, and was quickly picked to join the team. Hardly anything that would require superheroes ever happened here, so the Las Vegas Metro Police would hardly need them to intervene. It seemed to be a safe bet. The more she learned about Pyre and how his father had orchestrated all of this to keep him from getting drafted as well, the more she was convinced that her goals were in perfect alignment with the team.

"I'm glad I met you, Jim," Nicole said as they walked out of the arcade. She wrapped her hands around his arm and leaned her head against his shoulder. Jim understood her in ways that no one else ever had. Yes, he was still in high school, but he had also just turned eighteen recently, and was less than a year younger than she was. Everyone on the team was at least eighteen, due to laws regulating superheroes. Underage heroes' activities were severely restricted, limiting them primarily to training and support roles, rather than active heroics. She felt safe and comfortable with him, and could let herself relax with him in ways that she could never have done before with anyone else.

"Me too, Nicole," Jim said, reaching over and placing his free hand atop hers. He stopped when they were just outside the doors of the arcade, the lights and bustle of the Strip visible from where they stood, less than a block away. He turned to face her, then wrapped his arms around her. They kissed.

— § —

"Welcome back," the man on the television screen said, smiling. He wore a dark jacket and tie, and his dark brown hair was perfectly coiffed. "I'm Stanley Baxter for SNN Evening News. Since the debut of the Protectorate, there has been a spike in superhuman vigilantes."

The image on the screen shifted, and a photo of a caped man wearing a helmet with bug-like eyes appeared over Baxter's shoulder. "While their costumes may be flashy," Baxter continued, "federal officials stress that unsanctioned superheroics are illegal."

The image changed, this time filling the screen with recorded footage of an African American man standing at a podium. He was dressed in a dark business suit, and the podium bore a governmental seal. A caption appeared at the bottom of the screen, which read: Secretary Gavin Stevens, Department of Superhuman Affairs. "To all the would-be superheroes out there," Stevens said, "there's a better way. Register."

The image flashed back to Baxter in the newsroom. "Although the government hasn't yet pursued legal action against these unregistered heroes," he began, "Secretary Stevens stressed that, if necessary, his department will act."

Walter Campbell pressed a button on the remote, turning off the television. He tossed the remote onto the coffee table before him, where it clattered to a stop on the wooden surface.

"Something wrong," a man's voice called from the kitchen, "*Leafmaster?*"

Campbell groaned. He was never going to live that down. His boyfriend, a lanky young man with wildly unkempt hair and rough stubble on his jaw, walked into the living room of the small apartment that they shared, a drink in one hand and a sandwich in the other. His robe wafted around him as he walked, and he wore nothing else but boxer shorts and fuzzy slippers.

"Karl," Campbell began to protest as Karl dropped onto the couch next to him, his drink sloshing in his glass, but thankfully staying within it.

"What were you thinking," Karl asked, "showing up in that getup?" He shook his head, then took a bite out of his sandwich. As he began to chew, there was a knock at the front door. Karl's eyes went huge, matching his bulging cheeks, as he and Campbell both turned to look at the door.

Karl jumped up from the couch, making a beeline for the safety of the bedroom as Campbell rose to answer the door. Once Karl was in the other room, where he was most likely hastily getting dressed, Campbell opened the door. Standing at the doorway, Campbell found an older African American man in a gray suit. He smiled broadly, his bushy black mustache and hair showing hints of gray.

"Walt!" the man exclaimed. "My boy, I haven't seen you in ages."

"Hello, Mr. Davis," Campbell began as the older man pushed past him and entered the apartment.

"Call me Bobby," Davis insisted. "Your dad and I, we go way back."

"I don't know," Campbell hesitated, still holding the doorknob as he stood at the open door, "if I'm comfortable with that, sir."

Karl walked back into the room at that moment, now fully dressed and his hair combed. He stopped suddenly, and looked from Campbell at the door, to Davis, then back again. He blinked in confusion, but before he could ask any questions, Davis surged forward, grinning, his hand extended.

"Robert James Davis," the older man said, grabbing Karl's hand and shaking it vigorously, "attorney at law. Old friend of the family. And you are?"

"Um," Karl began hesitantly, "Karl Brown. I'm—"

"You must be Walt's roommate," Davis interrupted, then immediately let go of Karl's hand. "Pleasure to meet you." He turned back to Campbell, promptly ignoring Karl.

"Walt, my boy," Davis said, placing an arm around Campbell's shoulders, guiding him toward the small dining room table in the area adjacent to both the living room and the kitchen. "I spoke with your father, and he said that you are absolutely broken up about this whole superhero thing."

"Well, I—"

"Of course you are," Davis interrupted again. "Those corporations," he scoffed, "think they can just walk all over everyone."

"It's fine," Campbell insisted. "I didn't get the job, that's all."

"It's not fine!" Davis exclaimed. "You are grade-A superhero material, son! It's a travesty that they left you out!" Campbell looked pleadingly at Karl, who, bewildered, just shrugged, as if to say, *What can I possibly do?*

— § —

David Brown pulled into the parking lot at the visitors' center at the main gate of Nellis Air Force Base, which was located several miles north of the Strip. After Don had been arrested by the Security Forces policemen, he had been taken to Nellis, which was the nearest military base.

The entry to the base had a large area with red-colored rocks and a large, sand-colored sign atop similarly-colored bricks; the sign was decorated with the logo of the U.S. Air Force in brushed metal, with letters in matching metal that read U.S. Air Force, Nellis Air Force Base, Las Vegas, Nevada. A display of several stylized fighter jets flying in formation was behind the sign, arranged to look as though the jets were flying over it. In the distance, beyond the gate and the building next to it that housed the guard shack and the visitors' center, there was a roar like an explosion that just kept on going, and David could see the shape of a fighter jet rising into the sky. He wondered how anyone could live around the base with that much noise all the time, as he'd seen a number of apartment complexes and houses nearby as he drove up.

Stepping out of his car, David raised a hand to shield his eyes from the bright Nevada sun. He locked the car doors, and made his way inside. He'd come nearly every day for the past four days, hoping to see his brother, who was being held in the base's detention facility. They had finally relented on the second day, escorting him to a building several blocks inside of the base, past the large dormitory buildings that housed the junior enlisted airmen that were assigned to the various squadrons located at Nellis, as well as a hotel facility for visiting personnel, a cafeteria-style dining facility, and headquarters buildings for several of the squadrons.

The interior of the building was very much like a civilian police department, David had noted, though everyone wore camouflage instead of police uniforms. The military policemen—SPs, they had said they were called in the Air Force, for Security Police, which was a part of the Security Forces Squadron—led him into a small room with a table and chairs, and Don was led in several minutes later. The SPs stood by along the wall, near the small room's only door, while David tried to talk to his brother.

"Don," David said, "what were you thinking? Why would you try to attack me like that?"

Don just scowled, crossing his arms, and said nothing. He was wearing camouflage pants and an olive drab t-shirt, along with tan combat boots. It apparently was his uniform, or at least part of it, and David noticed that the pattern of the camouflage on Don's pants was a different color and style than the uniforms that the SPs were wearing.

David tried for almost twenty minutes, but Don refused to speak to him. No topic broke his silence: not the attack, their childhood, or their family. David finally left, frustrated, and the SPs escorted Don back to his cell. He hadn't come yesterday, but he was back again today, ready to try again. When he stepped inside the visitors' center, he was greeted by one of the sergeants on duty, whose nametape read "Phillips."

"Mr. Brown," Phillips said, approaching David. "I'm Tech Sergeant Phillips. Please, come with me." He escorted David into a small office within the visitors' center facility. Stepping behind the desk, which had a nameplate that read "TSgt Phillips" in the middle, and a computer monitor and keyboard off to one side, he remained standing as he turned to address David. Behind him on the wall were several plaques bearing his name, including one shaped like South Korea, another shaped like a shield, and one that looked like a large metal dish with American and Turkish flags. "I'm sorry, sir," Phillips began, "but your brother isn't here anymore."

David was both surprised and angry. No one had said anything about Don being moved yet. "Where is he?" he asked.

"He's been transferred back to his unit," Phillips said, "and is pending court-martial." He spread his hands apologetically. "I don't know anything beyond that."

"Look," David began, crossing his arms defiantly, "I—"

"He was only held here temporarily," Phillips interrupted, "because it was the nearest base." He pulled out a piece of paper from his desk drawer, then grabbed a pen and began writing. "He's back in Marine custody now." He raised the piece of paper in front of himself like a talisman. "Here's a number for his unit."

David snatched the paper from Sergeant Phillips' hand. He looked at it for a moment, reading the telephone number written on the paper, then turned and left the room.

— § —

"Dad!" John Chambers called out as he rushed through the door and into his father's office. He clutched a rolled-up newspaper in his hand, and wore a worried expression on his face. Stepping quickly over to his father's desk, John held the newspaper up so that Max could read the article that had gotten his attention. The newspaper headline, located at the top of page three of the Las Vegas Times, read "Leafmaster Sues Protectorate."

"Did you know about this yet?" John asked, trying to keep the panic out of his voice.

"Yes," Max replied. "I'm aware of it." To John's surprise, he didn't seem very concerned about the matter.

"What are we going to do about it?" John asked.

"*You're* not going to worry about it," Max replied, pointing a finger in his son's direction. "My lawyers can handle this." He paused a moment, leaning back in his chair. "Frankly, we expected this."

"You expected *this?*" John asked, incredulously.

"Not specifically," Max admitted, "but it was only a matter of time before someone litigated."

"And you're *sure* I'm the right person to lead this team?" John asked.

"Someone once told me," Max said, leaning forward confidentially, "'believe in yourself, and others will believe in you.'" He let his words hang in the air while John absorbed them. Before either could say anything else, the intercom built into the telephone on Max's desk buzzed.

"Mr. Chambers," a woman's voice said on the other end of the line, "Ms. Aeon is here to see you."

"Sorry, John," Max said apologetically to his son. "We'll talk later, okay?"

"Sure, dad," John replied. He was somewhat calmer than he had been when he entered the room just a few minutes earlier, at least, and Max's confidence had helped to bolster his own.

Max pressed a button on the telephone and said, "Send her in, Marcia." The door opened, and a striking woman with bright red hair and a finely-tailored gray business suit stepped through. She strode confidently past John, who stopped in his tracks, watching her as she walked toward Max's desk.

"John," Max said, his voice stern enough to catch the attention of his slack-jawed son.

"Wha—?" John began, snapping back to his senses. "Oh. Right. Later." John turned and left the room, closing the door behind him.

Once the door clicked shut, Max turned his attention to his guest, who had already taken a seat opposite from Max. "Now that we're alone, 'Ms. Aeon,'" Max began, trailing off expectantly.

"Now that we're alone," she echoed, "we can dispense with the pseudonym."

Max sat in his chair, and looked at her askance. "In exchange for yet another," he commented wryly. "Tell me, Tempora, will I ever find out who you really are?"

"In time," Tempora replied, a twinkle in her green eyes and a slight grin on her face.

Finished with the witty banter, Max went straight to business. "You could have warned me," he said, pointing an accusing finger at Tempora. "I could have had extra security—"

"No," she said, interrupting him and holding up a hand to stop him. "That would have made things worse."

Max sighed in resignation. He had first been approached by the woman who called herself Tempora nearly twenty-five years earlier. She had, from the beginning, been an enigma. She never seemed to age, and she always had an uncanny ability to predict the future. She had provided Max with business advice for as long as he'd known her, and she had never asked for anything in return until recently. That business advice had been the foundation of Max's—and his company's—rise to wealth and power, and in a very literal sense, he owed her everything.

"You've given me good advice over the years," Max began, "but I need you to ease my conscience."

"I haven't lied to you," Tempora replied, her tone and expression suddenly very serious. "Ever."

Max crossed his arms. "That's the only reason I founded the team like you asked."

"Then what's the problem?" Tempora asked, holding her hands out, palms upward, in a questioning gesture.

"I'm hesitant," Max admitted, "about putting my son in harm's way. And my ex-wife went through the roof when she found out about the team."

"Your son will be fine," Tempora said, smiling as she tried to reassure him. "And the team? They're going to save the world."

Chapter Four

The alert came while most of the team was gathered in the training center, though Psyche was the only member of the team not present, as she was attending a birthday party for her younger brother. In what Pyre now realized was a glaring oversight, the team had never developed a formalized training regimen. They were, instead, randomly shooting at targets with their powers. A useful skill, certainly, but nowhere near sufficient.

The team arrived at the site of the emergency, and everything went to hell almost immediately. The Las Vegas Metro Police Department was escorting a superhuman prisoner to McCarran Airport, for transfer to Stronghold Prison, a federal penitentiary in Arizona designed to house superhuman criminals, when the prisoner escaped police custody.

Five weeks had passed since the team's debut, and it had been two months since they had all been brought together for the first time in mid-January, and now that they were being deployed in the field for the first time, their lack of proper training was becoming—quite literally—painfully apparent.

The escaped felon was a man who called himself Radon. His powers had absolutely nothing to do with the radioactive gas, however; he simply thought it sounded like a cool name. Instead, he had a golden-colored metallic body, down to his hair, eyes, and teeth. His orange prison jumpsuit had been torn, and much of Radon's golden chest and arms were now reflecting the blinding afternoon sun every time he moved.

Nucleus, Singe, and Versipellis rushed toward Radon as soon as the team arrived on the scene. The prison transport van was overturned and lay on its side, steam rising from the cracked radiator, and gasoline pooling beneath a ruptured fuel tank. The pavement around Radon's feet was buckled and ruined, shattered chunks of asphalt forming into piles where the metal-bodied criminal struck the ground. An instant later, the three heroes suddenly stopped, as though they had run into a solid wall, though nothing could be seen.

"Crap!" Sphere exclaimed, then called out, "Sorry!"

As the three heroes picked themselves up from the ground, Radon lunged forward and slammed his fists into Versipellis like a pile driver. The shape-shifter had already assumed an armored form before entering the fight, however, and while the blow further shattered the pavement beneath Versipellis, it didn't harm him.

Versipellis swung an armored, razor-fingered fist at Radon, but the golden-skinned convict caught his wrist mid-punch, stopping the blow. As the pair grappled, Nucleus ignited clouds of plasma around his feet and hands, and launched himself into the air. Singe rolled to the side as Radon tried to stomp on her with his left foot, getting clear of the fight at the last instant.

Sphere rushed the fight, projecting a forcefield around himself. He readied a punch, backed with a forcefield around his fist, when Radon threw Versipellis at him. The shape-shifter collided with Sphere's forcefield, and the two heroes tumbled to the broken pavement.

"Form up on me!" Pyre called, to no avail. None of the team was listening to him, and they were all trying to take Radon down by themselves. Singe leaped onto Radon's back, but he grabbed her by the shoulders and threw her. The sparks from her hands ignited the pool of gasoline that had formed underneath the police transport van, and the flames spread quickly, engulfing the vehicle. She scrambled away, ready to rejoin the fight.

Sphere was on his knees at Radon's feet, holding his head, his eyes shut and his face screwed up in disorientation, and the villain was preparing to strike, his fists raised above his head. Singe leaped upon Radon's back, wrapping her arms around the golden man's neck and torso. Radon roared in anger, throwing his arms out to the sides, trying to dislodge Singe, when one of his fists struck Versipellis and sent him flying backward.

The shape-shifter landed hard and rolled into the flaming pool of gasoline. He screamed in pain. Pyre, who had been flying toward Radon from behind, Nucleus coming up alongside him, stopped and refocused on the fire. Using his pyrokinetic abilities, he willed the flames to dissipate. Moments later, the fire was out, but Versipellis held back, unwilling to return to the fight in his present condition.

Singe, enraged, began to pour electricity into Radon. An instant later, she began to scream, and her hair began to stand on end.

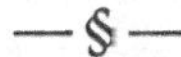

"It was horrible, mom," Pyre said the next evening as he sat on a large couch on the back patio at his mother's house in Beverly Hills. He had flown himself to see his mother after the botched events of the previous day, and he was recounting the events to her, still dressed in his uniform, which had been a more sensible choice for an impromptu flight from Las Vegas. "We charged in there, and he just tore us to pieces. He'd escaped from the police transport that was taking him to the airport. We tried to stop him, but it all just fell apart as soon as we got there.

"Nobody would listen to me," Pyre continued. "Everyone tried to stop Radon by themselves. When he managed to hurt Jim—Versipellis," he corrected himself, then paused, collecting his thoughts. After a moment, he exclaimed, "He had a metal body! What was she thinking?!" He held his head in his hands. "I don't know if I'm cut out for this."

"John," his mother, Jane Avery, said, leaning forward in her own chair, an arm extended to comfort him, "it's not your fault." Her blonde hair and blue eyes matched Pyre's own, but otherwise he was like a younger, more athletic version of his father.

"That's not the worst of it, mom," Pyre said, dropping his hands in front of himself as he continued to rest his elbows on his knees. "When Nicole died, I hit Radon with everything I had. I—I think I killed him." The image of Radon's metal body melting into a shapeless, golden puddle came unbidden to his mind.

Police reinforcements had arrived moments later, but it was too late for Singe. Her own electrical powers had been funneled back into her body, which had been in full contact with Radon's when she had unleashed her powers. The shock of the massive burst of electricity had stopped her heart, and despite the valiant efforts of the police officers and a team of paramedics who had arrived minutes later in an ambulance, they were unable to get her heart beating again.

John knew that it was his responsibility. He had been the team leader, and he hadn't made sure that they had trained for a fight like that. They hadn't trained to work together as a team. That was on him. Before he could say any of that to his mother, however, the air filled with a sound like fabric tearing. A breeze suddenly kicked up out of nowhere, knocking over the empty plastic cup that he'd finished drinking water from minutes earlier. The branches of the palm trees surrounding the property at his mother's home began to sway, and then a glowing, vertical red line formed in the air above the swimming pool in the back yard.

The line grew, glowing brightly in the dark, evening sky, stretching to nearly seven feet long, from top to bottom. An instant later, it began to widen from the center, and roiling, red clouds could be seen within. It was as if someone had ripped a hole in the sky, and revealed something *else* on the other side of reality.

A shape appeared at the center of the rip. Within moments, it resolved into a person. A woman. She had red hair, green eyes, and fair skin. She wore a lightweight gray jacket atop a green shirt and blue jeans. Pyre recognized her immediately. It was his father's enigmatic business partner, who he had seen so many times over the years when she had visited his office.

"You!" Pyre exclaimed. "I know you!" Clearly, she had super powers of some sort. Teleportation? Perhaps. But what was she doing here? Why was she here now? She floated from the rift in the sky and landed gently on the ground in front of Pyre, as the rift closed behind her. Telekinesis was apparently another one of her abilities.

"Call me Tempora," she said as she stepped forward to face Pyre. "I'm here to help you. It's vital that you remain with the Protectorate."

She knew. Somehow, she knew that Pyre had been considering leaving the team. "Why?" was all that he could manage to ask.

"It would be easier to show you," Tempora replied cryptically.

"He's not going *anywhere* with you!" Jane said forcefully, stepping forward and spreading her hands to drive home her opposition to the idea.

"Mom," Pyre said, "I recognize her. She's worked with dad before."

"Oh, believe me," Jane said bitterly, "I recognize her, too!" There was bad blood between Jane and Tempora that went back a very long time. Though she had never been able to prove it, Jane was convinced that Max had been having an affair with the young redhead. That had led to endless arguments, and eventually drove enough of a wedge between Pyre's parents that their marriage had ended in divorce when John was in middle school. Jane had returned to her home state of California, and the home that the couple had bought in Beverly Hills went to her in the divorce.

"No harm shall come to your son, Jane Avery," Tempora promised. Her tone softened, as she tried to assure Jane that she truly meant no harm. "The future still has much in store for him." The older woman just glared at her.

Tempora looked at the sky over the pool. A moment later, a new rift opened up, right where the old rift had been moments earlier. She looked back to Pyre. "Come with me," she said. "I will show you what you need to know. There is a storm coming. One that will threaten the entire world." She lifted gently into the air and floated back toward the rift.

Pyre looked back toward his mother. "I'll be all right, mom," he assured her, then rose into the sky as well, following Tempora. They flew through the rift, which sealed itself behind them.

Jeffrey Harlan

Chapter Five

The next day, Jim Williamson sat at his desk in his government class at North Las Vegas High School. He had drifted through his classes all day, unable to focus on any of them. While the fight on Saturday afternoon hadn't left any long-term physical harm, his world had been shattered by Nicole's death. In the two months they had been together, he had become closer to her than to anyone else he had ever known.

It didn't seem real, to not have her around anymore. Part of him still felt like he would be able to meet up with her again after he got out of school. That they could play video games at the arcade, or get some pizza, or watch a movie. But they couldn't. Not anymore.

His teacher, Mr. Shimasaki, had been talking about the effect of superhumans on the country's political systems over the decades, especially after their first appearance in the 1950s, but Jim hardly noticed. Shimasaki, to his credit, realized that Jim was in a difficult place at the moment, and was more than willing to give him the time he needed to process what he had just gone through. A combat veteran from the U.S. Army himself, Shimasaki knew some of the emotions that Jim was now trying to process.

Suddenly, an emergency tone began to blare over the school's public address system speakers. "Attention, teachers!" a voice called out over the speakers. "Code red!" Shimasaki's face fell, and worry furrowed his eyebrows.

"Mr. S," one of Jim's fellow students, an African American girl named Susan Leonard, asked, "what's a code red?"

"It's an emergency code," Shimasaki replied, fishing in his pocket for his keys as he crossed the room toward the door. "It means there's an attack on campus." He pulled his keys out and quickly sorted through them, searching for the key to his classroom door. "Gotta lock the door," he muttered.

"What *kind* of attack?" Jim asked, the situation having brought him back to the present. Before Shimasaki could answer, however, the door flew off of its hinges, slamming into him. He hit his head hard against the floor as he was sent flying, and was instantly rendered unconscious. In the hall on the other side of the doorway, a woman stood with her right hand extended toward the door. Her left hand held some kind of spear crossed with a scythe, and she wore a sword on a loose belt around her waist. She wore a plain white tank top, white running shorts, and a white corset. She had white leather vambraces around her forearms, and a pair of white socks and white running shoes on her feet. Her pale skin shone in the fluorescent light of the school's hallway, her blonde hair framing a thin face with narrowed, sky blue eyes.

Stepping past the fallen door, the woman entered the classroom and faced the two dozen students in their desks. She scanned the room, and her eyes locked on Jim. She hefted her spear, pointing it toward him, and announced, "Versipellis, I have come for you!"

Jim rose from his desk, and stepped into the open to face her. "What do you want?" he asked.

She hurled her spear at him. "Your head!" she screamed.

Jim shifted his form, opening a hole in his torso, where the spear would have impacted. He quickly shifted tentacles around it and grabbed the shaft with his hands, stopping it before it could travel further and potentially harm one of his classmates. Fortunately, they had taken the opportunity to start evacuating the classroom, and two of the stronger boys were already carrying the unconscious form of Mr. Shimasaki toward the door.

"Yeah," Jim said, dropping the spear to the floor. "Good luck with that. Your aim sucks, by the way."

"Wait," the woman said, suddenly confused. "I can't sense you! I was drawn to this room by a powerful superhuman..." She trailed off, scanning the other students in the room. Her eyes locked on one of the escaping students, who was following close behind the boys who were carrying their teacher. "It's her!" the blonde woman cried, pointing at Susan.

"Lady," Jim said as he shifted his clothing into his superhero uniform and stepped between Susan and the woman, who had drawn a sword and was pointing it menacingly in their direction, "you've got a few loose screws. You're reading me and think it's her!"

"I can sense if someone's a superhuman," the woman said. "It draws me like a magnet. And if they die when I'm near, I get their abilities!"

"You said you couldn't sense me," Versipellis retorted, "so your radar must be off."

"Oh, no," the woman said, shaking her head and smiling confidently. "I'm not wrong, and I'm going to prove it!" She unsheathed the sword and raised it into a fighting stance.

Versipellis began to shift into his armored form, his hands becoming razor-sharp, red claws. "Bring it, crazy lady," he said as Susan gasped behind him.

"Both of your heads will be mine!" the woman screamed. She raised her sword to her shoulder and began to lunge toward them to attack... and collapsed to the ground, the sword clattering loudly beside her. She looked up, eyes wide. Versipellis turned, and saw Susan standing behind him, an arm extended toward the psychotic killer, her expression one of fury.

The woman shot up into the air, and slammed into the ceiling. Then she fell to the ground with a crunch, as the linoleum tiles shattered and the concrete floor beneath cracked from the impact. The woman bounced between the ceiling and the floor several more times, then came to a rest, floating in midair. Susan stepped forward, holding a hand up in concentration.

"I knew," the woman said between pained gasps, "I was right."

"Leave," Susan said angrily. "And never come back here again." She turned her hand, pointing her palm toward the white-clad woman. An instant later, the woman shot through the air, shattering the window as she rocketed through it. She continued to soar into the distance, her form growing smaller and fainter within seconds before disappearing toward the horizon.

Versipellis turned, wide-eyed, to look at Susan, whose expression had suddenly gone from angry to saddened as soon as the sword-wielding woman was gone. "Susan," he began, "that was incredible!" He noticed the change in her demeanor. "What's the— oh. *Right.* Look, nobody saw you use your powers. Nobody else has to know."

"I," Susan began, then hesitated. "Thanks."

"Why don't you want anyone to know you're a superhuman?" Versipellis asked. "What you can do is amazing!"

"I'm afraid," Susan admitted, ashamed. "Of getting drafted. Or being attacked, like today. Just because of my genetics. I don't want that kind of life."

Versipellis pondered her reply for a moment, then nodded. Stepping into the hallway outside of the classroom, he stopped and turned to face Susan. He placed both hands on her shoulders and looked into her eyes. "However you want to handle this," he said, "you have my full support."

"Let," Susan began, then stopped. She considered her words, then began again, "Let me think about it, okay?"

"All right," Versipellis nodded. "The press and the cops will be here soon. As far as they're concerned, that psycho came here to attack me, and you and the rest of the class just got caught in the crossfire."

Susan smiled. "Thank you," she said. They turned and made their way toward the exit. As Versipellis had predicted, the police and news vans were pulling into the parking lot as they stepped outside.

The news crews swarmed Versipellis even faster than the police could get to him, demanding to know what had happened. He raised his hands, palms outward, and waved for them to step back. He briefly summarized what had happened, that an unidentified superhuman woman had attacked him, but that he had fought her off, and she had fled the premises. Fortunately, his teacher had come around, and no one had been seriously hurt in the attack.

"Who attacked you?" one of the reporters called out, as a half-dozen microphones were pushed toward his face. Just as many video cameras pointed at him, carried on the shoulders of the camera crews that joined several of the reporters. It was disconcerting, being the focus of so much attention, and Versipellis wasn't used to it.

"I don't know," he replied. "She never said who she was. She just showed up in the middle of class and tried to kill me." He paused, frustrated at the situation, then continued, "She attacked me at *school*, man. What's up with that?"

"Versipellis!" called another reporter, an Asian woman that he vaguely recognized from one of the cable news networks, vying for his attention. When he glanced in her direction, she took that as a cue, and continued, "There have been calls for superhuman students like yourself to be transferred to schools that are better equipped for your... special circumstances. In light of this attack, can you blame them?"

Versipellis was dumbstruck for a moment, caught off-guard by the question. He recovered quickly enough, however, and replied, "This was an aberration. Just because someone has super powers doesn't make them any less deserving of the same education as anyone else. I'm going to graduate in a few months. Should I have to uproot to a new school just because I've got powers? I've been a student here for years without problems."

Another reporter stepped forward, speaking over the previous woman before she could continue with her line of questioning. "Do you know why," he began, "you were attacked today?"

Versipellis nodded, making eye contact with the male reporter. "Yeah," he replied. "She said that she could absorb other people's powers if they died around her. She wanted to kill me and take my powers." He almost added, "the psycho," but managed to stop himself. A petite, raven-haired Latina stepped behind Versipellis and placed a hand lightly on his shoulder. She smiled for the cameras, then began to address the gathered reporters.

"I'm Angelica Bernal," she began, "the vice principal here at North Vegas High." She glanced briefly at Versipellis as she continued, "I want to express my deep gratitude to Mr. Williamson—I mean, Versipellis," she corrected herself, "for his quick thinking to safeguard the lives of his fellow students. We will be coordinating closely with the Las Vegas

Metro Police Department in regards to this case, and there will be no further questions at this time. Thank you."

Bernal stepped back, moving an arm to guide Versipellis away from the reporters. Despite her assertion that she would not be taking any further questions, several of the reporters, led by the woman who'd badgered him about segregated schools for superhumans, Versipellis noted, continued to call out questions to them. Ignoring them, Bernal led Versipellis back inside the building.

"How are you holding up, Jim?" Bernal asked, once they were alone in the empty hallway. "I heard what happened on Saturday on the news. I'm so sorry."

Versipellis smiled thinly, nodding. "Thank you, Mrs. Bernal," he said. "I'm doing okay, I guess. I'm just," he paused. Finding words for what he was feeling right now was hard for him. "I'm just getting through my day."

Bernal placed a reassuring hand on his shoulder once more. "I understand," she said. "If you need someone to talk to, my door is open."

Versipellis nodded, then he and Bernal both turned their heads toward the sound of the doors leading to the building's exterior opening, then closing once again. They saw a khaki-clad police officer begin to walk toward them. He had close-cropped brown hair, and a bushy mustache to match.

"Excuse me," the police officer said as he approached the pair, "but I'll need to take your statements on what happened."

CHAPTER SIX

Pyre followed Tempora into the rift, which hovered in the air above the swimming pool in the back yard of his mother's home in Beverly Hills. He wasn't sure what to expect when he passed through the rift, though he anticipated from the red, swirling clouds that he could see that there would be some sort of intermediary space between his mother's house and wherever it was that they were going.

Instead, the moment he flew through the rift, he was temporarily blinded by intense light. One moment, it was dusk in Southern California. The sun had almost completely set, so aside from a faint reddish glow near the horizon, the only illumination came from the lightbulbs in his mother's home. The next moment, he was blinking back tears as he found himself instantly under the midday sun.

Pyre held a hand over his eyes for some temporary shade as his vision adjusted. The air was salty and humid. It smelled of seawater, and it was warm with a light breeze. He settled to the ground, where green grass swayed in the breeze, and dirt and rocks crunched under his boots.

As his eyes adjusted, Pyre joined Tempora. The tall redhead was standing a few feet ahead of him, on a bluff overlooking a beach. The waves crashed along the coast, and Pyre saw some birds flying overhead, though he noticed that something about them seemed odd. They drifted lazily among the clouds in the azure sky, but they looked far larger than any seagulls he'd ever seen, and their feathers were dark colors, rather than white.

Along the coast, far in the distance, he could see what looked like a small village. The buildings looked like they were made of a mix of an adobe-like clay and some sort of rough glass. The hut-sized buildings were conical, almost like ceramic and glass tipis. Pyre had never seen anything like them. He could see the vague shapes of people walking among the buildings, but they, too, looked odd. They bobbed when they walked, and they all leaned forward all the time.

"Where *are* we?" Pyre asked, finally breaking the silence between him and Tempora.

"The Yucatan," Tempora replied, "about sixty-five million years ago."

Pyre blinked, and stared at her, mouth agog. Surely he had heard her wrong. "What?" he finally asked, incredulous, after several moments.

"Humanity wasn't the first intelligent life on Earth," Tempora replied matter-of-factly.

Sixty-five million years. It was the end of the Cretaceous Age, the last age of the Mezozoic Era, the final age of dinosaurs. *Intelligent* dinosaurs? Was that what he was seeing in the village?

"What happened?" Pyre demanded.

Tempora pointed to the sky. "Extinction," she said, simply. Pyre's gaze followed her arm. Faintly, among the clouds, he could make out a glowing smudge. He'd seen it earlier, and dismissed it as some kind of cloud, but it was bigger now than just a few minutes earlier.

Wait, he thought. *Sixty-five million years ago...*

"Is," he began uncertainly. "Is that...?"

"A comet," Tempora confirmed. "*The* comet."

Pyre's stomach dropped. Somehow, she had the ability to travel through time. She had taken him here, to not only show him that there had been primitive, tool-using dinosaurs who built their homes with clay and glass, but that they had been wiped out by the same comet that killed off the rest of the dinosaurs.

Why would she show me this? he wondered. *What does this have to do with why I should stay with the team?*

"There's more that you need to see," Tempora said as another rift opened. As the rift stabilized, Pyre once again followed Tempora through. This time, he closed his eyes just as he passed through the rift, hoping his vision would adjust faster to whatever difference there was in the lighting on the other side. Emerging on the other side of the rift, he immediately noticed that the air was colder, wetter, and it reeked of thick, choking smoke.

He slowly opened his eyes, and saw that he and Tempora were standing in an alleyway in a city, though he couldn't yet place which one. It was nighttime, wherever it was that they were now, and he could hear a cacophony of voices and sounds coming from the street at the end of the alley.

The ground was paved with cobblestones, and it was littered with garbage and scraps of wet newsprint. Small puddles dotted the ground. Rats, roaches, and other vermin darted in and out of the shadows, scurrying about in search of food and safety from predators, and drinking from the puddles. Everything had a layer of black soot. Tempora led him to the mouth of the alley, but held back, just far enough to see out to the street beyond, but not so far that they might draw attention.

"London," Tempora announced. "1862." She pointed out, toward the city beyond the end of the alley. "Look up."

Pyre looked out. People in mid-nineteenth-century clothing walked on the sidewalks and across the streets. Horses drew carts, wagons, and carriages, their hooves clopping loudly on the cobblestone streets. Lamps filled with whale oil burned overhead, thick black smoke rising from their sconces as they provided dim yet serviceable light against the evening's darkness. Dark clouds of coal smoke filled the air, and he could see pillars of the thick, oily smoke rising from factory smokestacks along the river.

In the distance, perhaps half a mile away, he could see the clock tower at the houses of Parliament that held Big Ben. At this distance, and with the thick greenish-black fog of pollution, Pyre could barely make out the enormous clock face, which was lit from within, and he could see that it was 8:15 p.m. He also noticed a glow emanating from the thick clouds above the famous clock tower. Were it not 1862, like Tempora had said, he would have sworn that an aircraft of some sort was flying low and slow through the clouds. But aircraft wouldn't be invented for decades, and the kind of running lights that could produce that amount of lighting would be several more decades beyond that.

A shape slowly emerged from the clouds, and pillars of light that were every bit as bright as stadium lighting pierced the blackness of the night sky. The source of the lights all but hovered, moving impossibly slow for an object of that size, in the air above Big Ben. The craft was enormous, hundreds of yards across, and made of a gleaming metal. As people began to take notice of the craft, voices turned into shouts and screams. Hands pointed at the massive, metal saucer that came to a rest above Big Ben.

"Time to go," Tempora said, stepping back from the mouth of the alley. The air began to move, paper and garbage whirling about, as another rift opened behind her and Pyre, deeper into the alleyway. He looked back at her, words failing him as he pointed in mute astonishment and horror at the flying saucer.

"We must leave," she reiterated, "while everyone's attention is elsewhere. There is more to show you." She stepped through the rift, which hovered inches above the alley's cobblestone pavement, and vanished. Glancing back to the spectacle unfolding in the London sky, then to the rift, Pyre began to run. He leaped through the rift, not wanting to risk having it close, stranding him nearly one hundred fifty years in the past, and he immediately found himself in freefall.

Using his ability to fly, Pyre stopped his plummet toward the ground within seconds. Hovering, he looked around, hoping to orient himself, when something roared past him. Following the enormous blurred shape, he saw, receding into the distance, a P-51 Mustang fighter plane.

The P-51 banked, the roar of its propellers receding but nonetheless deafening. He noticed now that he could hear the sound of other planes, as well as the staccato beat of the machine guns mounted in their wings.

"Central Europe," Tempora said, flying up beside him in the cold night air. "1944." Before he could ask how the Second World War factored into what she was showing him, another large metal object shot past them in the sky. Unlike the P-51s, however, this was completely silent, and shaped like an inverted dinner plate.

"The pilots called them foo fighters," Tempora explained. "The term 'UFO' wouldn't be coined for a few more years. None of them knew what they were; just that they were fast, silent, and they didn't show up on radar." They watched the dogfight as it receded into the distance.

Another rift opened before them, and Tempora passed through it without a word. Pyre followed, confused but intrigued. He found himself near the ground in a desert at night, and in the distance, he could see large, flat mountain formations—mesas. They had to be in the Southwestern United States; that was the only place that he knew of where mesas existed. He settled to the ground next to Tempora, the rocky surface crunching beneath his boots.

"1947," Tempora announced. "Roswell, New Mexico."

"You mean," Pyre began, stunned once again, "that really happened?"

Tempora pointed into the distance. "It's about to happen," she replied. "Over there." Pyre followed her arm, and he could see a point of light moving in the night sky. Suddenly, storm clouds materialized out of seemingly nowhere. One moment, the sky was relatively clear, with only thin, patchy clouds in the distance, and the next, a bank of thick, dark storm clouds rolled into existence, as if in fast forward on a video.

A lightning bolt cracked from the clouds, striking the moving point of light with a deafening boom that reached their ears a moment later. The clouds began to dissipate as quickly as they had formed, and the object began to wobble, then plummeted to the ground.

As the object fell from the sky, it drew closer, and Pyre was able to make it out more clearly: it was one of the smaller flying saucers, like he had seen engaged with the dogfight with the P-51s over Europe moments ago for him, and three years ago for the rest of the world.

The flying saucer slammed into the ground, digging a trench in its wake as it slid across the desert floor, dirt flying everywhere. When it finally settled to a halt, one end pointed into the night sky at an odd angle, and the other end was buried in the ground.

Motion and a glimmer of light caught Pyre's attention in the distance. He could see two people, but they were too far away for him to make out any details. Then he realized that one of them was wearing a long, white cape atop a black outfit, and his hand was crackling with electricity.

The first superhumans appeared in late 1952, at the end of the Korean War. That was still five years away, and the first costumed heroes and villains didn't appear for another year after that.

"Um," Pyre began, pointing at the pair in the distance, "who is that?"

"We should be going," Tempora said, clearly avoiding the question. She wasn't telling him something about what was going on, which was ironic, given that she was taking him on a tour of history to share information about some pretty massive secrets.

"What are you hiding?" Pyre demanded.

Tempora ignored his question once again. Instead, she said, "The Army is on its way." Without any further comment, she opened another rift, and stepped through. Pyre stormed through after her in frustration. He forgot to close or cover his eys this time, however, and he was again blinded by sudden daylight. He held up a hand to shield his eyes, wincing in discomfort. As his vision returned, Tempora stepped over to his side.

"Los Angeles," she said. "Three months into your future. Look up." Pyre saw that he was, indeed, in Los Angeles. And hovering above the skyscrapers of downtown Los Angeles was an enormous flying saucer, identical to the one he had seen over London in 1862, if not the very same one.

"This is an invasion," Tempora said, then corrected herself. "No, an *extermination*. Centuries of planning, all leading to this." Pyre stared, the horror growing as he finally understood the context of what he'd been shown. *This* was why he couldn't leave the team? How could that have any impact on this?

"There's," Tempora began hesitantly, as she placed a hand on Pyre's shoulder and continued, "more that you need to see." She opened another rift and stepped through. Pyre followed, and as he stepped through, he could swear that he heard a familiar voice calling his name. When he passed through the rift, however, he was instantly cut off from whoever had been calling for him, just as instantly as he began having trouble breathing.

The air was thick with smoke, worse even than it had been in London, and as he looked around, he saw enormous pillars of thick red smoke rising into the sky. The ground, too, was barren, reddish-brown dirt, and the sky itself was tinted red, though Pyre couldn't tell if that was from the thick clouds of smoke pooling above him, from the setting sun, or perhaps even from a combination of the two. The vista was apocalyptic, and he could see no signs of life anywhere around him. The air was thick with red smoke, and Pyre gasped for breath.

"My god," he breathed.

"This was their last victim," Tempora said, standing several feet behind him, giving him room to take in the all-but-literal hellscape around them.

"This isn't Earth?" he asked in astonishment.

"No," Tempora replied. "This is Mars."

"Mars is uninhabitable," Pyre said. "I've seen the photos!"

"It wasn't always," she explained, "and if you leave the Protectorate, Earth will suffer the same fate." There it was: her reason for showing all of this to him.

"Why?" he demanded. "What is so special about me? How do I prevent this from happening to Earth?"

"I can't tell you that," she replied with a sigh. "I wish I could, but knowing too much about the future could risk changing it from how it's supposed to happen."

"Isn't that exactly what you're doing?" Pyre asked.

"I'm guiding you," she said. "You still have to make the decisions." A rift opened next to Pyre. "I've shown you all that I can. It's time for you to go back home, now." She indicated the rift. Pyre looked at the rift, the dust and smoke flowing around it. He turned back to Tempora. He had so many questions.

A sad expression crossed her features, and he felt a force shove him toward the rift, and an instant later, he was back at his mother's home in Beverly Hills.

— § —

Sensors plunged into the pool of golden metal. It was held in a large basin labeled "Warning: Hazardous Material" in large white letters on a red background. Two people in white lab coats observed the material, which rippled slightly around the points where the sensor probes had been inserted.

"So he's not dead?" asked the woman with chocolate-colored skin, and hair drawn back into a severe bun, whose golden earrings matched the material in the basin.

"The metal hasn't hardened," the other person with her, a bookish man with thick glasses, pale skin, and dark brown hair, replied, consulting the clipboard in his hand, "and we're reading neural activity."

"Brr," the woman shuddered. "Weird."

"Tell me about it," the man replied, setting the clipboard back down on the countertop near the basin, which held the liquefied remains of one convicted criminal known as Radon. "Hey," he said, changing the subject and making his way toward the door, "it's lunch time!"

"You buying?" the woman asked, following her companion out the door.

"You wish," the man replied as the door shut behind them, leaving the room in near silence, save for the beeping of instruments set to monitor Radon's remains.

Remains that began to bulge, then formed a thick tentacle that reached up and out of the basin. It angled slightly at the end, looking almost like the top of a periscope on a submarine, and the tentacle moved around, as if examining its surroundings. After a moment, it withdrew into the basin, once again becoming a formless mass of golden metal.

CHAPTER SEVEN

Private First Class Donald Bryton, perhaps best known to the public as Plasmid, sat in his semi-dress uniform at the defense table in a military courtroom at Marine Corps Base Camp Pendleton, which was located north of Oceanside, California. To his right sat his attorney, a young Marine lawyer in the Judge Advocate General, First Lieutenant Teresa Maxwell. She was a few years older than Private Bryton, having graduated from law school and entering the Marine Corps as a lieutenant a year earlier. Her black hair was pulled into a severe bun, her makeup was impeccable, and she sat rigidly straight in her chair, her case file arranged neatly before her.

At the table across the aisle from them sat the prosecutor, Captain Shawn Dunlop. Somewhat older, Captain Dunlop had served as a JAG prosecutor for several years. Like everyone present, he was dressed in his olive drab semi-dress uniform, albeit with far more ribbons than either Private Bryton or Lieutenant Maxwell, owing to his longer service and greater experience. His posture was alert, but less rigid than Maxwell's.

There were only a handful of people seated in the seats behind the defense and prosecution tables. Among them was David Brown, a superhero known as Nucleus and a member of the Protectorate, a team of superheroes from Las Vegas. The grandson of the first superhero, the first to be called Nucleus, Brown was also the half-brother of the defendant.

The judge, a large African American man who kept his dark-skinned head shaved due to emerging hair loss, wore a traditional dark judge's robes atop his own semi-dress uniform. He tapped his gavel, bringing the proceedings to order, and Private Bryton and the attorneys all stood.

"Private First Class Donald Bryton," the judge, Major Salim Abdi, began, "you have been found guilty of all charges. This court will now pronounce sentence." He paused, and looked directly at Bryton. "Due to the circumstances, and a request for leniency by an aggrieved party," he glanced momentarily at Brown in a seat two rows behind Bryton, "I offer a choice, Marine: dishonorable discharge, and either twenty years in a military prison, or a new start at the colony on the moon, where you will likely never set foot on the Earth again."

"Your honor," Lieutenant Maxwell began, caught by surprise by the judge's unexpected offer, "I'd like a moment to confer with—"

"I choose the moon, sir," Bryton, impulsive as always, said, interrupting his attorney.

"One moment, your honor," Maxwell said, nonplussed. She turned to Bryton and said, "Private, we need to weigh your options." She turned back to Judge Abdi. "Defense requests a short recess, your honor."

Abdi nodded. "Court is in recess and will reconvene in fifteen minutes." His gavel made a cracking sound as it struck the plate at the front of his desk.

—§—

The Protectorate gathered together in uniform. It was the first Saturday in April, and they had gathered for their weekly training session. Today was different, however. For the past month, ever since Singe had died during a botched mission to escort the superhuman criminal known as Radon to McCarran Airport for transport to Stronghold, a federal prison for superhumans located in Arizona, a pall had fallen over the team. Media coverage had been scathing, and regulatory agencies that ranged from the local police oversight commission to the U.S. Department of Superhuman Affairs had taken an interest in the team's training regimen.

As a result, the team's training sessions were getting an overhaul. An experienced mentor was brought aboard, both to smooth over public relations and to give the benefit of decades of experience to the team. Today was his first day, and he eyed the team warily. He had white hair and despite his advanced age of 83, he was nevertheless powerfully built.

"Boys and girls," he said, folding his arms, "I'm Percy van Norton. Sixty-some years ago, I was one of the world's first superhumans. People called me Strongman." The young heroes assembled before him nodded; he was a legend, and they all knew exactly who he was. Of them, Nucleus was perhaps best acquainted with him; his grandfather, the original Nucleus, was not only the first superhero, he was also close friends with van Norton. "Word is," van Norton continued, "there's a storm coming. I'm here to teach you how to survive it."

Van Norton's story was well known to the young heroes. He was not only one of the first superheroes in history, he was also the first to go public with his identity. As a result, his entire life quickly became well-known, including the details around how his powers first manifested, when he was a soldier in the Korean War.

— § —

"Merry freakin' Christmas," Corporal Cliff Roberts said. He shivered and tried to zip his fiberglass-lined uniform parka higher, but it was already zipped as far as it would go. He adjusted his scarf so that it covered the lower half of his face, and his rubber "Mickey Mouse" cold weather boots, so nicknamed because of their bulky shape, squeaked as he walked on the frozen dirt. His M1 Garand rifle began to slip from his shoulder, and he grabbed the strap and hefted it back up against his ruck. Once the wooden stock of the rifle was back in place, he shoved his hands back into his pockets, his breath freezing into clouds as he muttered his intense disapproval of the Korean winter weather.

Private First Class Percival "Percy" van Norton, overhearing Corporal Roberts' muttered invective regarding the weather, struggled valiantly to contain his laughter. While Roberts hailed from the warmer climes of California, van Norton was a native of New York City, and thus well acquainted with cold winters. It was cold, to be sure, at a temperature very near freezing, but not so bitterly cold that van Norton felt the need to complain about it... yet.

The Korean War had been raging for more than two years, though none of the generals or politicians would call it a war; they used terms like "conflict" or "police action." Whatever they called it, people had been fighting and dying for years, and as far as van Norton was concerned, it was a war. Van Norton had been fighting in it for just over a year now, having been drafted in November 1951 at the age of eighteen, and he was more than ready for it to all be over so that he could go back home. He missed home: Christmas with his family, baseball games at Yankee Stadium, summers at the Hamptons, and spending an evening at the movies with his girl of the moment.

His thoughts were interrupted when a Willy's Jeep shot past him. He watched the vehicle bounce over the rough path that they laughingly called a "road," which his platoon was marching North on, toward communist-held territory. As it passed the front of van Norton's unit, there was a terrible explosion, and the jeep suddenly flipped into the air, dirt spewing from the ground that had been underneath it mere moments before. Time seemed to slow as van Norton watched in horror at the spectacle before him. The sergeant driving the jeep was thrown into the air, his helmet flying from his head and his arms pinwheeling at his sides, the angle at which he was ejected from the jeep's open passenger compartment sending him flying headfirst toward the ground. Meanwhile, the jeep spun twice in the air before slamming back down to earth. It rolled to a stop, pinning the now-unconscious sergeant beneath its shattered steel mass.

Adrenaline surged through van Norton's veins. As his brothers-in-arms took shelter, not knowing yet if the explosion was due to a land mine or enemy fire, van Norton ran toward the smoking hulk of the jeep. He started to pull at the bottom of the jeep, but before his mind could process what he was doing and tell him that there was no way that he could lift the vehicle by himself, he astonished himself by suddenly and effortlessly lifting the entire jeep above his head. Van Norton's mind raced. These jeeps weighed more than half a ton, yet it felt as though it weighed no more than a few pounds. He had always been strong, but never like this.

He stared in disbelief at the jeep above his head, then glanced down at the unconscious sergeant at his feet. He heaved the weight forward, intending to drop the metal hulk safely away from the wounded sergeant, only to watch in shock as it sailed far into the distance. He looked incomprehensibly at his hands. A shuffling noise to his side drew his attention, and he saw the other men in his platoon staring at him with looks ranging from astonishment to horror.

Versipellis held the enormous block over his head. His biceps bulged, having grown larger with added muscle mass so he could lift the heavy object, which was made of metal and weighed several hundred pounds. He prepared to throw the block, and looked for a target. At that moment, Psyche struck. She pushed with her telekinesis, shoving Versipellis out from under the block and into a nearby wall in the training facility.

The block, however, didn't move with the young shapeshifter, and would have crushed Sphere, who was nearby, if he hadn't raised a forcefield bubble around himself at the last instant. The block bounced off of the forcefield, and landed on the ground with a dull thud.

"Stop!" van Norton called over the training facility's speakers. He was watching from the observation booth as the team as they went through a battle drill that he had devised, with the team's roster divided into two groups. "You're not working like a team." He sighed, realization dawning that the young heroes needed far more rudimentary training than he'd anticipated. "I'll be damned if I let another one of you get killed because of it. Get cleaned up. We're starting over from scratch."

An hour later, the team assembled in the training facility once more, now showered and changed into regular street clothing. In the intervening time, van Norton had put together a makeshift classroom, with a half-dozen chairs facing a rolling whiteboard along one of the room's walls.

"Sit down," van Norton instructed. As the young heroes took their seats, he continued, "Welcome to basic training." He looked at his students, took a breath, then began, "You're called in to assist the police with a superhuman attacking the Strip. What is your primary objective?"

"Beat the bad guy," Sphere, aka Kevin Burke, said with a chuckle.

"Wrong," van Norton said immediately. Noting the confused looks on the team's faces, he continued, "Your objective, first and foremost, is to protect the public. Evacuate civilians. Contain any threats. Once the public is safe, then yes, take the bad guy down. Quickly, so he can't do any more harm."

— § —

Kevin quickly swapped out the books in his backpack for a new set from his locker as John "Pyre" Chambers stood nearby. Four days had passed since their first day of training with van Norton, who had insisted on daily training sessions, rather than the weekly sessions they'd held in the past. Each day had started with an hour of classroom instruction, with topics ranging from squad-level tactics to the law as it pertained to state-sanctioned teams of superhumans, like the Protectorate.

"I swear," Kevin muttered, "Strongman's trying to kill us."

"He's trying to get us ready," John replied as Kevin closed the door of his locker.

"Right," Kevin said, his voice dripping with sarcasm as the pair began to walk down the nearly-deserted hallway. "For an alien invasion."

"This is serious, Kevin," John said.

"Sorry, John," Kevin said, "but I find that stuff a little hard to swallow."

"I know what I saw," John insisted.

"Do you?" Kevin asked. "How can you be sure?"

"I've seen that woman most of my life," John replied. "Now that I know she's a time traveler," his voice trailed off for a moment as he gathered his thoughts. "It explains a few things."

The pair entered a classroom just as the bell rang. "Like what?" Kevin asked, continuing their conversation as he and John took their seats.

"All those years," John replied, "she never seemed to age. Now I know why."

Their teacher cleared his throat, his hands on his hips as he stood nearby. "If it's all right with you two gentlemen," he said dryly, "I'd like to begin class now."

Chapter Eight

Don Bryton lay on his back as a pair of technicians tightened the straps securing him to his seat. One of them placed a foot on his shoulder for leverage as he pulled, and the strap dug into Don's upper body. The technicians checked him over, and once they were satisfied, moved on to the person in the seat next to him, repeating the procedure.

Don looked around. He was in the passenger compartment of a relatively large space capsule, which was on the launch pad at Cape Canaveral, Florida. Once he agreed to be sent off to the moon, everything went into motion fairly quickly. His dishonorable discharge from the Marine Corps meant that he would be ineligible for any kind of veterans' benefits, but he honestly didn't care about that; he'd never wanted to be in the military in the first place. That paperwork was finished in a matter of minutes, and had clearly been prepared well in advance of the sentencing hearing.

The next day, he was taken under guard to Los Angeles International Airport, and escorted onto a plane by a taciturn MP. He was dosed with dampening gas every two hours from the moment he left Camp Pendleton until after he arrived in Florida, where he was transferred to the custody of the NASA crew that oversaw his accelerated orientation program. There was a launch scheduled exactly one week after his sentencing date, and they had that time to bring him up to speed on everything he would need to know about his life going forward.

The passengers were all strapped tightly into their seats in a matter of minutes. All of their meager belongings were secured in a cargo compartment elsewhere in the capsule long before they came aboard. None of them had much; documents, photos, videos, and the like had all been converted and stored digitally to save space and mass, and clothing was kept to a minimum. At the moment, they all wore identical gray jumpsuits, like pilots and astronauts had worn for decades.

The technicians exited the capsule and sealed the hatch. Don could hear the light hiss of the life support system's fans circulating the air. Minutes passed in silence that was broken only by the occasional muted conversation between some of the passengers and by the radio chatter between the spacecraft's pilots and mission control, which was broadcast through the earbuds they all wore. Just as Don decided to take a nap while he waited for liftoff, the countdown began. The capsule began to vibrate as the engines ignited.

"...three," the voice of a man in mission control said through the earbud, "two... one... liftoff!"

The capsule bucked as the rocket began to rise into the air. The acceleration shoved Don into his seat with even greater force than he had expected. His breathing grew ragged and labored as he struggled to adjust to the change in the force of gravity pulling against him.

"You all right?" the young man in the seat to his right asked. He was Asian, from California judging by his accent, and he looked concerned. He was clearly struggling with the force of acceleration as well, but less so than Don. "You're the new guy they just added a few days ago, right?"

"I'm fine," Don replied through gritted teeth.

"We'll be in zero g in a couple of minutes," the young man assured him. "Then it's three days to the moon."

— § —

The days passed in relative monotony. Don kept to himself, though several of his fellow passengers attempted to engage him in conversation. He spent most of his time floating near one of the observation windows in the passenger compartment, watching the moon grow steadily larger as the days passed.

He had a lot of time to think. He had ruined his own life, he finally realized. All that time, all those years, he had blamed his brother for his misfortunes, but David could never have caused them. His parents had cared more about themselves than about him. He had never been a priority in their lives.

As they neared the moon on the third day, the spacecraft flipped around. Inertia kept them moving steadily toward the moon, and now the windows faced Earth. It was so far away, and looked so small. Don's heart began to ache as he realized that this was, effectively, the beginning of a life in exile, and he was unlikely to ever set foot on his home planet again.

Returning to his seat at the flight crew's direction, he and the others buckled themselves back in. The seats had doubled as beds during the flight, keeping them safely secured in place while they slept in zero g. Now, like with the takeoff a few days earlier, it would cushion them against the force of deceleration and keep them from being flung across the compartment. Soon, the pilots would fire the ship's engines in order to slow their approach, and they would land at Armstrong Lunar Base.

The colony was first founded twenty years ago, shortly after President Clinton's reelection for his second term, and coinciding with the twenty-seventh anniversary of the Apollo 11 moon landing. Part of Clinton's election campaign for his first term was a return to the moon, echoing the legacy of his idol, President Kennedy. Some groups also saw it as a way to reassert human achievements after four decades of the existence of superhumans, and the program gained unexpected support from otherwise disparate groups. Not one to look a gift horse in the mouth, Clinton took support where he could find it, and four years later, humans returned to the moon for the first time in decades.

The colony started small. At first, it was just a handful of capsules sent in unmanned landers, which were then assembled by the early astronauts. The first group didn't even stay permanently, as they were replaced by a new group of astronauts after three months. The rotations continued, however, and new modules were constructed. Two years later, construction began on the colony's most ambitious project to that point: a complex located largely underground, and insulated with regolith that was harvested from the area around the nascent colony. Construction took a year, most of which was spent digging out the trench that became the complex's interior.

That complex was now their destination. Over the past decade, it had been slowly expanded, with new tunnels and levels added. Work was underway on a second major expansion, with a giant trench being dug near the location of the first complex. Don had learned that his role at the colony would be as a laborer in the construction crews working on the new complex, and over the next year or two, it would become a mirror of the original complex. On the other side of that mound of regolith, which was dotted with a handful of small openings for windows and airlocks, as well as a massive observation window that overlooked a park within, a landing pad had also been constructed, where the spacecraft traveling to and from Earth, as well as smaller craft designed to traverse the lunar surface, could park and be serviced in between missions.

Once the spacecraft settled onto the surface, the passengers were given the all-clear to unbuckle their restraints. The light gravity was an unusual sensation. Objects stayed in place when you put them down, but everything felt significantly lighter. Don pulled out a tablet from the small drawer under his seat. He held it up, then dropped it. It slowly drifted down, and he grabbed it again a moment later, returning it to the drawer.

Most of the other passengers stayed in their seats. Some pulled out their tablets and began to read, others engaged in conversations. Don sat and watched them, silently. A few minutes after the ship had landed, he heard a metallic thump as a transport vehicle attached to the airlock at the base of the ship. He and the other passengers waited as the ground crew transferred their belongings from the cargo compartment into the transport. The minutes stretched into a boring eternity as they waited for the announcement that they were cleared to leave the passenger compartment and move into the transport vehicle. Once they left, the interior of the ship would be cleaned, the waste tanks emptied, and the ship refueled for its return to Earth.

Don had spent a great deal of time during the trip reading the manuals that had been provided for him on his tablet. He knew that the colony recycled literally everything, up to and including human waste; feces were used as fertilizer for plants that provided food and helped to recycle the air, and urine was processed to purify and reuse the water, while the remaining elements were broken down for use elsewhere. The idea unsettled him somewhat, but it made sense.

The transport brought them into a large airlock, which was just slightly larger than the vehicle itself. The door sealed behind them, and pressurized air rushed into the room. Within minutes, the pressure was equalized with the that in the interior of the colony. The interior door opened in front of the transport, and they continued in, to a relatively cavernous loading bay.

As the colonists exited the transport, once it had parked, they were led into a passenger terminal not unlike what one might find at a small airport. A group of people was waiting, and they began to greet the individual new arrivals. A large, intimidating man stepped up to Don. His expression was neutral, yet serious. His demeanor screamed "security."

"Mr. Bryton," the man said. It wasn't a question. The records of everyone aboard the capsule had been on file, and they knew exactly who he was. They'd had weeks to prepare for his arrival. "Follow me, please." The large man turned, and stepped gingerly away, toward a door at the far end of the room.

Don stepped to follow, and launched into the air. He smacked his head into the ceiling. Wincing and grabbing at his skull with both hands, he began to settle back to the ground. He swore he could hear a snicker come from the security man.

Stepping more lightly to compensate for the lower gravity, Don followed through the hallways to a section of offices. A secretary met him, and led him through a door, while the security man waited outside.

Don over-corrected his step, and the back of his head slammed into the top of the concrete door frame. Rubbing his head once again, he took a seat in one of the chairs offered to him across from a plain desk that occupied most of one side of the room. The desk appeared to be made of ceramic composites, and was painted to look like wood, but wasn't entirely convincing. If anything, the desk's top reminded Don of the desks he'd had in high school, albeit on a larger scale. Photos lined the walls, chronicling the first moon landing by the crew of Apollo 11: Buzz Aldrin and the colony's namesake, Neil Armstrong.

A man sat on the other side of the desk. He had a pale complexion and dark brown hair, and he looked like he was in his mid to late thirties. On the wall behind him, a portrait of Neil Armstrong and a photo of Buzz Aldrin walking on the lunar surface flanked a much larger photograph of the Earth rising above the surface of the moon, which had been taken from orbit by the crew of Apollo 8.

"The gravity does take some getting used to," the man acknowledged as Don rubbed the back of his head once again. Don recognized his face from a portrait in the briefing materials that he'd been provided with, and the name plate on the desk confirmed it: this was Martin Jefferson, the administrator of the colony. He was, essentially, the town's mayor and the top of the governmental food chain for a couple hundred thousand miles.

"Welcome to Armstrong Colony, Mr. Bryton," Jefferson began. "Your paperwork is in order, and a room has been prepared for you."

"You mean my cell," Don said. No one else on his flight was getting the personal attention of the top dog; his conviction and exile here had clearly warranted him special treatment.

"No," Jefferson replied, "I mean your *room*." He paused to let that sink in: he was offering Don a second chance, not as a prisoner, but as a colonist, just like everyone else that had come here with him. "Let's be honest," he continued amiably, "we're on the moon. Where would you escape to?"

"In other words," Don said, "we're all prisoners here."

"In a manner of speaking," Jefferson said, moving to sit on the edge of his desk near Don, to highlight the informality of the meeting, "yes, I suppose so."

"But my sentence," Don began to protest.

"Doesn't mean much here," Jefferson replied. The door opened once again, and a young woman stepped in. She had dark brown skin and her jet black hair was cut in a simple bob style and held back with a red headband. She nodded to Jefferson as she entered, but stayed near the doorway.

"I'll hand you over to Michaela," Jefferson said, indicating the new arrival. "She'll help you get settled in."

Don followed the young woman into the hallway. She led him through a few corners, and at the end of the latest hallway, Don could see an enormous open space. They reached the end, and found themselves on a walkway that overlooked a cavernous opening at the heart of the colony complex. Enormous windows showed the lunar surface beyond, outside their sealed environment: "beautiful desolation," as one of the Apollo astronauts had described it.

Below the windows was a sprawling, park-like area filled with grass, trees, and even a large pond. People relaxed in the park, and walked along paths that crisscrossed the open space; Don could even see a couple having a picnic, seated on a blanket on the grass, with a basket of food and drinks at their feet. Several stories up, the ceiling was painted a light blue, like an artificial sky, and floodlights shone upon it to reflect diffused light in artificial daylight.

"What's that?" Don asked in surprise.

"The Central Gardens," Michaela replied. "It's a nice place to relax and see some green."

"I wasn't expecting so much open space," Don admitted.

"People need open spaces, Mr. Bryton," Michaela said.

"Call me Don," he said.

"All right," Michaela replied. "Don." She raised an arm, indicating for him to follow. Michaela led Don down to the main level, pointing out the restaurants that had been set up, as well as recreational facilities located just off the Central Gardens, which she noted had been nicknamed "Armstrong Central Park" by some of the colonists. Leading him deeper into the complex, she pointed out the more traditional cafeteria facilities, a laundry facility, and more places that he would need to know about.

After an hour, she led him to a series of hallways lined with doors that reminded him of nothing so much as a hotel. She stopped at one of the doors. Like every door in the colony, it had a tag that labeled it with an alphanumeric code that served as an address. This door, however, also had a second tag underneath that, which read, "Donald Bryton," and a viewfinder lens underneath that.

"Well," Michaela began, turning to face him, "this is your room, Don." She opened the door, and he could see the bag with his belongings resting on the foot of the bed, which was in the far corner of the room. There was a small desk built into the wall near the head of the bed, a small set of shelves built into the walls above and beside the desk, and a set of dresser drawers underneath a pair of doors that had to be a closet along the wall near the door. As he stepped inside, he saw a second door along the wall at the foot of the bed, which he guessed must lead to a bathroom.

"I'll leave you to get settled in," Michaela said from the doorway, and she left.

Chapter Nine

Percy van Norton stood behind his commanding officer in the office of the colonel commanding the American forces in the area. It was 1968, and, thanks to the Superhuman Induction Act, he'd been recalled to military service, and he was now in Saigon.

"Sir," his commanding officer, Captain Tod Holton, said, "let us go out there!" Holton was the most recent commanding officer of the elite joint service special forces unit, Team Liberty, which was comprised almost entirely of superhumans. Holton was also the third to hold the title of Captain Freedom, and he had a square jaw, black hair, and boyish good looks. He was a from a small Midwestern town called Valleyville, where his high school sweetheart, Barbie, still waited for him.

"I'm sorry, captain," Colonel Luke Stewart said. Stewart was seated behind his desk, and was flanked by the flags of the United States of America and the U.S. Army. He was an older man with a gleaming bald head and a strip of short, gray hair that wrapped around the sides of his head. "I can't authorize that."

Captain Holton spread his arms in frustration and said, "Superhuman troops could end this war in a month!" Van Norton, now sporting the stripes of a Sergeant First Class, was one of Team Liberty's senior non-commissioned officers. He and the other sergeants assembled with him behind Captain Holton nodded their agreement. To van Norton's left was Marine Gunnery Sergeant Lawrence "Ferro" Nichols, a Black man whose skin had been permanently turned to a dark metal. Behind Nichols stood Army Staff Sergeant Luis "Brainpunch" Marquez, a Puerto Rican man with telekinetic abilities. Standing behind van Norton, Air Force Sergeant Daniel "Eagle" Peterson kept his enormous, almost stereotypically angelic, wings tightly folded against his back, lest he accidentally bump into something in the crowded office.

Stewart held up a hand, quieting Holton. "Congress made its position clear, captain," Stewart said. "We can only use superhumans if the enemy does so first."

"Then what, sir," Holton began, "is the point of drafting all the superhumans, if we're just going to have them sit on the sidelines?"

"After the Russkies parked those nukes in Cuba," Stewart replied, "what else could Congress do?"

The military had been inundated with superhuman soldiers over the last several years, following the passage of the Superhuman Induction Act in late 1962. While only a small fraction of them were ultimately picked to serve in Team Liberty, the others had all been transferred to units that weren't involved in the fighting in Vietnam. For the same reason that the use of nuclear weapons had been removed from consideration in the conflict, the use of superhuman soldiers was likewise barred: escalation. The concern in Congress was that, should either nukes or superhumans be used, the Soviet Union would enter the conflict directly, and the long-dreaded Third World War would finally erupt. Experts believed the same consideration was currently preventing the North Vietnamese forces and their allies from deploying their own superhumans.

"I maintain," Holton argued, "that this is strategically inadvisable, sir."

"For what it's worth," Stewart said, leaning back in his chair and crossing his arms, "I agree, captain."

— § —

Van Norton crossed his arms as he leaned back against the wall and faced the assembled members of the Protectorate.

"You're not going out there," he said, "until I say you're ready."

"And just how long will that take?" Sphere demanded.

"As long as it takes," van Norton said, his tone brooking no arguments. "Now, since you're all in uniform and ready to go anyway, report to the simulator room." None of the young heroes moved. Instead, nearly all of them glared angrily at van Norton. While he sympathized with their desire to go out and do good as heroes, he knew all too well what could happen to the unprepared. Tragedy had already struck this team, and he would make sure they would be better prepared in the future.

After a moment, Pyre finally broke the silence. "Come on, guys," he said. "Let's go." Reluctantly at first, the others turned and followed him out the door.

Once the team had left the room, van Norton exited as well, and made his way to the observation and control room that overlook the team's training facility. When he'd first met them, he could see the seeds of a strong leader in Pyre, but the young man was troubled and plagued with uncertainty. That was, at least, beginning to fall away, and van Norton could see that he had the potential to be a great leader in time.

He had been briefed on the more... incredible aspects of Pyre's story: how a time traveler had shown him a secret alien invasion, which was due to occur in just two months' time. The others had assumed that his lack of incredulity at the claim stemmed from a life full of incredible experiences. While that was true, the specifics were even stranger than they had realized. They were also strictly and highly classified to this day. He wasn't surprised by the tale of an alien invasion in the works, because he already knew about it.

Van Norton saw the team had assembled in the room below, and he started one of the training scenarios he'd programmed into the simulator. As he watched, the door to the room behind him opened once more. He continued to watch the team through the window, and listened as the door closed once again, and footsteps crossed the room.

"How are they doing, Mr. van Norton?" Max Chambers asked as he stepped up beside him.

"Better," van Norton replied, noting Max's presence out of the corner of his right eye. "I think they're nearly ready."

Max blinked. "Why haven't you told them that?"

"No way," van Norton harrumphed. "They'll get cocky, and the last few weeks will have been for nothing."

Don Bryton had an itch on his chin. Normally, that wouldn't be an issue, but he was in a spacesuit on the surface of the moon. Taking off his helmet to scratch that itch could have fatal consequences. Fortunately, the designers of these suits had decades of real-world experience to draw from, and they'd installed a small piece of velcro on the inside of the helmet. Don leaned his head forward, and rubbed his itching chin against it. Relief was immediate.

Don refocused his attention on the rock in front of him. While the rest of the work crew that he was with had both industrial construction equipment and hand-held tools to excavate the area and clear the rock, Don had his own powers.

The way his powers worked, however, meant that he was unable to create a plasma in the vacuum of space. That left two options to utilize his powers, and they'd set up equipment to make it possible for him to use both. The first option simply involved enclosing him and whatever surface he would be working with inside a portable, sealed environment bubble. Once inside, Don could use the atmosphere within to generate his plasma, which he could shoot at the rocks to break them up. The other option, which he was now testing out for the first time, involved a specially modified set of gauntlets on his hardened space suit. The gauntlets had an independent supply of gases that he could ignite.

To his great surprise, it was working perfectly. The hardest part so far had been in figuring out how to blast the rocks without having the debris from the explosion ricochet back and strike his suit. The first time, he stood directly in front of his target, and was instantly showered with a hail of debris. Fortunately, his suit was reinforced and armored for mining operations, but it was safer to minimize repeated strikes if possible.

Now he stood at an angle from the rock face, and several yards away from his target. He clicked the buttons built into the palms of his suit's gloves twice in rapid succession, activating the flow of reactant gas from the emitters at the ends of the gauntlets around his forearms, then activated his powers, igniting the gas into a glowing plasma. He took aim and fired, projecting a stream of plasma at the rock face. He bored a small trench into the rock face, then shifted position and carved another. The two trenches joined beneath the surface of the rock, and the section of the rock between them sheared off, shattering into fragments in slow motion as it struck the ground below. His supply of reactant gases was limited, so he shut off the flow, which would prolong the time he had before he needed to return and swap out reactant gas cylinders.

—§—

His shift over, Don returned through the airlock with the rest of his construction detail. The others all laughed and joked as they removed their spacesuits. Don placed his own in his locker, carefully stowing his specialized gear until he would need it again the next day.

He showered and changed, dressing in a comfortable Henley shirt and jeans that he had brought with him from Earth. As he left the locker room, he found Michaela waiting for him.

"How was work?" she asked.

"Not bad, actually," Don admitted, grinning, "once I figured out how to blast the rock without it shooting back at me." They started walking toward the common areas at the heart of the complex.

"Just be careful," she admonished, "to get all the rock dust off of you. Without erosion, that stuff is razor sharp and can really mess up your lungs."

Don nodded. That was something his supervisor had stressed as well. The entire crew was sprayed down with high-powered air jets in the airlock to remove any loose dust from their suits, and the showers were meant just as much for removing any additional dust transferred onto their skin while taking off their spacesuits as they were for cleaning away the sweat and grime of the day's labors.

"So," Don began, changing the topic slightly, "I know the construction project is making a big expansion for the colony. I was wondering, though, what's the area we're digging going to be used for?"

The pair stepped into the vast open area of the Central Gardens. A tension Don hadn't even realized he was feeling lifted as he saw the open "sky," which he realized was now shades of red, pink, and orange, rather than the blue he'd seen before.

Michaela saw how the expression on his face had suddenly relaxed when they stepped into the open area, and she gave him a moment to take it in before she answered. "A new habitat section," she said a few moments later, "so we can bring in more colonists for the new jobs the rest of the expansion will be opening up."

Don nodded. He and Michaela walked through the Central Gardens together in silence for a few moments. His stomach growled, and he noticed that one of the restaurants along the perimeter of the Central Gardens that he'd been wanting to go to was nearby.

"I was about to get dinner," Don began, turning his head to look in Michaela's direction. "Care to join me?"

"Sure," Michaela said, smiling.

Don led her to the restaurant he'd been looking at, and her eyes widened. It had a large entryway that led directly onto the Central Gardens, and one of the large oak trees was planted near the entrance. Within the restaurant, several small tables, just large enough to seat two or three people, were decorated with white tablecloths and simple floral arrangements.

The concierge led them to a table at the center of the dining room, and Don noticed that there were no other diners present. *Maybe it's just early,* he thought.

They sat, and Don checked the menu. He had been craving a steak since before he left Earth, and this was the only steakhouse on the moon. He and Michaela made some idle small talk as they ordered and waited for their food. They discussed their day at work, and Don learned that she worked in the colony's hospital.

"How long have you been a colonist here?" Don asked after their food had been brought out to them. His steak looked as good as it smelled, and it was covered in butter and spices. A generous portion of mashed potatoes and vegetables accompanied the steak. It was expensive, even more so than it would have been on Earth, but it was worth the indulgence as far as he was concerned.

"I signed up as a medical assistant," Michaela replied, "about three years ago. I'm nearly finished with a nursing program that I'm taking through correspondence, and I'll be an RN soon."

"That's great," Don smiled. "I didn't know you could do that."

"It's been hard," she admitted. "Online classes were hard enough without the transmission lag from here to Earth and back. Two and a half seconds doesn't seem like much until you're trying to have a conversation with your professor. The doctors and nurses I work with have been a huge help."

"I'm glad to hear that," Don said. "You have any family?"

"No," Michaela replied. "Only child. My parents are back on Earth, but," she paused for a moment before continuing, "well, we didn't talk much even before I came here." She shook her head, as if trying to shake off the thoughts in her head. "How about you?" she asked, finally.

Don fell silent, the piece of steak on his fork hovering inches away from his mouth after his hand stopped mid-bite. After a moment, he replied, "A half-brother."

Michaela gasped in regret as she realized her mistake. Don's story was well-known, as it had been all over the news a few months earlier. "Oh," she said, her hand over her mouth. "I'm sorry. I didn't think. I should have realized—"

"Don't worry about it," Don said. "He's on Earth, and I'm here." He put the piece of his steak in his mouth, closing his eyes in pleasure at the taste and texture. He chewed slowly, savoring his meal.

Michaela gently touched his hand. "I'll try to avoid that subject, okay? It's a sore spot, and I completely understand. Let's talk about something else." She got a gleam in her eye as she grinned. "Like how it's a pretty ballsy move to take me to the most expensive restaurant on the Moon as a first date."

— § —

John "Pyre" Chambers dropped the comic book to the floor in disgust, groaning loudly as he reclined on the couch in the entertainment center that had been set up for the team in their headquarters complex at the Chambers Casino and Resort in Las Vegas. Kevin "Sphere" Burke turned to look at his friend, distracted from the game of pool he'd been playing with David "Nucleus" Brown.

"What's wrong, John?" Kevin asked.

John held his head in his palm and lamented, "This comic book about us is terrible!"

Danielle "Psyche" Thompson looked up from the book she'd been reading at the window, the setting sun casting the horizon beyond in shades of red, pink, and orange. "It can't be *that* bad," she said.

John picked up the comic from the floor by his side, then began to read dramatically, "'Back, foul villain! You shan't stop Pyre!'" He groaned again, then said, "The artwork is super sexist. There's no way you could stand like that without throwing your back out, Dani. It even has Nicole calling me hot... head..."

John trailed off, realizing the effect even mentioning their fallen teammate's name had on Jim "Versipellis" Williamson, who was playing video games on a custom-made arcade cabinet nearby. Jim paused a moment, his head dropping.

"Jim!" John exclaimed in horror at his *faux pas*. "I'm... I'm sorry, man! This was written before—"

"Don't sweat it, John," Jim replied quietly, returning to his game. "Not your fault."

"Guys," Dani interrupted. She paused until she had everyone's attention, then continued, "It's snowing!" Everyone rushed to the window, where they could see heavy winds pushing the palm trees, and the sky was dark and overcast, obscured by the frozen precipitation.

"That's not just snowing," John said in astonishment. "It's a blizzard!"

"In *Vegas?*" Kevin asked, incredulous. Even seeing it through the window, directly in front of him, it was hard to believe.

"We interrupt this broadcast," the well-groomed news anchor said on the screen of the television, "to bring you this special report." The image changed away from the man at the news desk, and the face of a large African American man filled the screen. The way the image was framed and how it shook, it had clearly been filmed with his phone.

"I am Weathercaster!" the man shouted into the camera. His hair was styled in tightly braided rows, and his facial hair was trimmed into bushy mutton chops. He wore a black outfit with a white cape. "Give me a billion dollars, or I destroy Las Vegas!" The image cut back to the news anchor, sitting at a desk with his co-anchor, an Asian woman whose hair was pulled into a large, loose bun.

"Brr," she said, adding a fake shiver.

"Scared, Amy?" the anchor asked.

"No, Stephen," she said, "just cold!"

The pair laughed for a moment, then the anchor, Stephen, said, "We go now to our weatherman, Rene Skeyes—"

Chapter Ten

We're stopping this fruitcake," Pyre said as he zipped up the front of his uniform, his gloves in his left hand as he pointed," whether you like it or not." He stood at his locker in the men's locker room as he dressed, Sphere and Nucleus at their lockers nearby, dressing quickly in their own uniforms. Psyche had gone off to the women's locker room, which she had to herself, as she was currently the only woman on the team, and Versipellis' shapeshifting powers allowed him to change into his uniform in an instant.

"Are you now?" Percy van Norton asked, his arms crossed as he leaned against the door of the locker room.

Pyre and the others, now fully dressed in their uniforms, stepped past van Norton and into the hallway, where Psyche was waiting for them with Versipellis.

"We're the only ones who can," Pyre said with determination in his voice. The five young heroes briskly made their way to the rooftop access that was easily afforded by the location of their headquarters; it had been heavily modified from the penthouse suites at the Chambers Casino and Resort, and an entire wing of rooms on the floors below.

Stepping into the stormy evening, half-melted snow crunched and squeaked under their boots. Pyre tapped the activation key on an earbud nestled into his right ear as the team formed up around him.

"Dispatch," he announced, "this is Pyre. The Protectorate is en route to the warehouse address that you provided."

"Copy, Pyre," a woman's voice replied over the earbud. She was a dispatch operator for the Las Vegas Metro Police Department, and her job this evening now involved coordinating the team's deployment as part of the overall emergency response effort during the current crisis. "Police, fire, and EMS are en route as well."

Pyre leaped into the sky. Moments later, the rest of the team followed suit: Psyche propelled herself via telekinesis, Sphere by surrounding himself in a forcefield bubble that moved under his mental command, Nucleus on a jet of plasma, and Versipellis by growing a set of giant, leathery, red, dragon-like wings out of his back.

Van Norton watched the team recede into the storm-darkened evening sky, leaning against the doorway that led from the roof back into the team's headquarters on the floors below. He grinned.

"Good hunting, kids," he said.

Despite the strong winds and freezing weather, the team made good time, and within minutes reached the warehouse on the south end of the city that the Metro Police had identified as the source of the recording that Weathercaster had posted online. Pyre had learned from the dispatcher that he'd spoken to over the phone earlier that the new, would-be villain had neglected to turn off the feature on his phone's camera that embedded his GPS coordinates into the metadata of every photo and video that he took. Finding him had been child's play.

The team touched down behind the line of police vehicles and cops that was forming across from the entrance to the warehouse. The police officers were shivering from the unexpected cold weather; it was spring in Las Vegas, and they had all switched over to their short-sleeve uniforms as the temperatures had risen once again.

The team made their way through the police barricade, and into the warehouse. Pyre led them in, his fists ablaze for both illumination and as a ready defense. They found a table set up in an open area near the door, and a laptop computer was set up and running on the table. Psyche suddenly looked to her right just as Sphere shot forward to access the computer.

"Guys!" Sphere called out. "Over here!"

The warehouse exploded as a massive bolt of lightning came down from the clouds above and struck a container of anhydrous ammonia used for cooling the massive facility.

As the dust began to clear, Pyre lifted himself from beneath the rubble. He stood, and another lightning bolt struck him squarely in the chest. He fell to the ground, eyes wide and unblinking, as Weathercaster stepped over his smoking body.

The villain kicked Pyre's still form with a sneer, then looked at the overcast skies above. The clouds began to swirl, and condensed into a funnel. That funnel grew, and within moments, an enormous tornado touched down at the south end of Las Vegas Boulevard, better known as the Las Vegas Strip, and began to rip the iconic buildings and signs to shreds. People, animals, cars, and debris were hurled skyward in an orgy of destruction.

Weathercaster grinned wickedly, surrounded by a forcefield bubble. Sphere stood a few feet away from the villain in the warehouse.

The entirely intact warehouse.

"I've got him now," Sphere said, his arm extended toward the villain. "You can drop the illusion, Psyche."

Weathercaster spun, looking around in confusion as he suddenly found himself back in the real world, and Psyche slumped forward with a groan. Projecting a convincing reality into Weathercaster's mind while the rest of the team gained the moments they needed to react had drained her. Pyre was at her side in an instant, helping her to stay on her feet.

"Easy, Dani," Pyre said reassuringly. "The cops are here now." As if on cue, several officers clad in the khaki uniforms of the Metro Police entered the area, their weapons drawn and ready. "You did great," he added.

She had sensed Weathercaster's presence, waiting for them as they had entered the warehouse, and knew he had planned to strike. Quick thinking, thanks in part to the weeks of training they'd recently received, allowed her to put him into a trance-like illusory state, though she would take a great deal of time to recover from the effort.

Sphere opened a hole in the forcefield surrounding Weathercaster for a split second, allowing the MPD officer to drop a canister of dampening gas, which Sphere then sealed in with the villain an instant later. He waited a few minutes for the gas to take effect, and the team stepped back to a safe distance. The police officers moved in, guns drawn and ready, and Sphere dropped the forcefield. The gas began to dissipate once the atmosphere within the bubble rejoined that of the world outside, and Weathercaster thrust an arm toward the police officers.

Nothing happened.

The police officers closed the circle. Weathercaster tried to fight, but they quickly overwhelmed, subdued, and handcuffed him. They led him outside, and placed him in the back of one of the waiting squad cars, while the officer in charge took Pyre's statement on what had just happened.

Weathercaster scowled as the patrolman maneuvered him into the back seat of the police car, the man's hand pushing his head down so that it wouldn't hit the top of the car's door frame. The cop, a young white man with light blond hair, shut the door once he was satisfied that Weathercaster was secure, and stepped over to join his colleagues, who were taking statements from the members of the Protectorate.

Weathercaster struggled against the handcuffs that bound his wrists uncomfortably behind his back in the back seat of the car. He felt a breeze, and looked up to see a woman seated next to him in the car. He blinked at her in confusion. She had red hair, pale skin, and wore a gray jacket over a green shirt and blue jeans.

"Weathercaster," Tempora began without preamble, "I have need of your abilities."

He harrumphed and replied, "They used dampening gas."

"It will wear off," Tempora said. "We have time." Weathercaster sniffed derisively, and began struggling against the handcuffs once again. "Let me help you with that," Tempora said. With a click, the cuffs suddenly fell away.

Weathercaster eyed her warily as he held his arms in front of himself once more and flexed his fingers. "We're surrounded by cops," he said. "How you gonna bust me out of here?"

Tempora smiled, and Weathercaster found himself falling. A moment later, he hit the ground. He looked around, and saw that they were in a desert, somewhere.

"Teleporter, huh?" he asked, picking himself up and brushing dirt from his cape.

"Not exactly," she said.

"So whatta ya need me to do?" he asked. "And where are we?"

Tempora smiled again. "Welcome to Roswell," she replied. "You're about to give humanity a fighting chance to survive."

The image on screen flickered as the video file played. It stabilized, and David Brown could see the image of his brother, Don Bryton. He looked far more calm than he had the last time they had spoken, more than a month before.

"Um, hi, David," Don's image said, and he waved weakly at the camera. He dropped his head for a moment, then looked back at the camera. "I'm sorry for what I did. I was so angry, but for the wrong reasons. I've had a lot of time to think, and I'm ashamed of what I did. I wanted you to know that. I've got a second chance here." He paused, and smiled. "There's this girl, too." He trailed off for a moment, then his expression turned serious. "Don't let me screw this up." He shook his head, then continued, "I should let you go now." His hand filled the screen, then the image went to static for an instant before the video file ended.

David sat back in his chair, pondering what he'd just seen. Someone cleared their throat behind him, and he turned to see Percy van Norton.

"Mind if I join you, son?" van Norton asked.

"No," David said, then immediately corrected himself. "Yes. I mean, sure. Er... gah! Come in." Van Norton chuckled as he stepped through the open doorway and into the former hotel room that now served as temporary quarters for David. Each member of the team had their own room in the facility, where they could stay overnight if needed.

"Your grandpa and I," van Norton began, "we went way back. Served in Korea together." He paused. "Well, sort of. We were in Team Liberty together at the end of the war. After the war, he became the first super-hero. Convinced me to be his partner." *Another stretch*, he admitted to himself.

Van Norton sighed. "I wish to God I could have prevented his death. He never got to see your mom born." Another memory, this time of the funeral, came, unbidden, to van Norton.

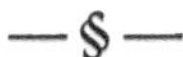

"This way, sir," the usher said softly as he held the door open for Strongman to enter the church. Cameras flashed and snapped behind him. He stepped through the door, and he saw it immediately.

The casket, placed on a pedestal in a small room to the side of the church's main hall, was surrounded by flowers. There were wreaths in stands on either side of it, with other arrangements in pots and vases lined up beside them and in front of the casket itself. Dozens of people were seated inside. A few of them, like himself, wore brightly-colored uniforms, albeit adorned with black armbands to mark their period of mourning for the loss of one of their own; they were superheroes and members of the Minutemen, New York's team of superheroes, and one of their founding members was no longer among them.

Some of them still had secret identities, insofar as the public didn't know who they were under the mask, though they had to register their identities with the state in order to join the team and enjoy the benefits they were afforded under the law. In order for them to attend what had become a highly public funeral, they decided that they would attend in costume. As a show of solidarity, Strongman did so as well, even though his identity had been public for years.

Moving to the front of the room, he found his friend's widow, struggling to hold back tears as she sat in front of the coffin. Strongman sat next to her and put an arm around her shoulders. She leaned over and rested her head on his shoulder. As though given permission, she began to sob, and buried her face in the fabric of Strongman's tunic. He wrapped his other arm around her and held her as she finally allowed her grief to flow. He felt something poke him, and realized that the baby she was carrying had just kicked him. It should have been a happy moment. Nucleus should have been here.

He looked to the casket that held his friend, that would forever hold his friend. They couldn't even have an open casket funeral, because his body had been so ravaged. One of the gangs had somehow managed to capture him. They had tied him up, then shot him in the head, and dumped his body in the river. By the time he had been found, decomposition had begun to set in. He had been the one to identify the body; the police had recognized the uniform, but he knew the face under the mask. It was not how he ever wanted to remember his friend, but he feared he would never be able to sear the image from his memory.

Shaking off the recollection, van Norton placed a hand on the shoulder of his late friend's grandson. "I'm glad you took on his mantle," van Norton said after a moment. "He'd be proud." He paused again before continuing, "Your brother's made mistakes. Big ones. But if he can get it together, there's still hope for him yet."

— § —

On the moon, two men in spacesuits worked to repair a damaged regolith harvester. The lunar soil was valuable in that it could be processed for a number of raw materials, and it could also be converted into concrete bricks for construction on the expansion of the lunar base. The tank-like tread on this harvester had been damaged, however, when a large rock had been caught in the gears, causing the tread to come apart.

The two men, Joe Lieber and Jack King, were maintenance engineers known for their creative solutions that helped keep the colony running. They passed tools to one another, working diligently to get the giant machine back into operation. As King held two ends of the broken track together, Lieber spun a ratchet to tighten a new bolt that would rejoin the ends.

The sun was high in the sky behind them, providing ample illumination for their work. Without warning, however, everything suddenly went pitch black, and the only light now came from the relatively pitiful glow of the lamps built into the sides of their helmets, which came on automatically in the darkness.

Lieber shot a confused look at King, who simply shrugged. From his position holding the ends of the tread together, he couldn't see what could have suddenly blocked the sunlight and cast them into shadow, nor could he turn to look without letting go and undoing all of their work. Lieber nodded, indicating that he was going to turn around to see what was going on. As he turned, his jaw dropped.

Passing slowly overhead, obscuring the sun, was a massive space-craft. It was easily a mile across, made from a reflective silver metal, and shaped like a stereotypical flying saucer.

Chapter Eleven

The news helicopters circled overhead, the sound of their rotors a low, thrumming drumbeat. They were low enough to the ground that the desert sand kicked up into the air in small whirlwinds. At the heart of the artificial windstorm, a blonde woman in white stood, armed with a sword held at the ready. Surrounding her in the desert just outside of Las Vegas, the half-dozen young heroes of the Protectorate stood, ready to take her into custody.

This woman had attacked Versipellis at school two months earlier, but had been driven away by the shapeshifting hero and his classmate, Susan Leonard. She had claimed at the time that she had the ability to absorb the powers of any superhuman who died near her, and she wanted to take Versipellis' powers for herself. Now she was back, and more dangerous than ever.

"The first power I ever absorbed," she said, raising her sword over her head and parallel to the ground, "was precognition. I've seen what's coming. It can't be stopped. I've got to be prepared. That future is almost here, and I need power—*your* powers—if I'm going to survive this apocalypse."

"Lady," Versipellis said, his body shifting into an armored red form, "you are out of your damn mind."

"Sphere, contain her!" Pyre ordered, pointing at the woman. "Graviton, hold her down!" Before they could react, however, they began to clutch at their throats, choking, as they levitated several inches above the desert floor. Sphere kicked wildly to no effect, and Graviton, the team's newest addition, did the same.

Graviton—whose uniform featured light blue fabric on the shoulders, sleeves, and legs, with dark blue piping to accent it—was Versipellis' classmate, Susan Leonard, who had also been a target in the blonde woman's attack on their school. Possessing the ability to manipulate gravitational fields, she had hoped to keep her powers a secret. After realizing the near-impossibility of that desire, she then elected to join her classmate in the Protectorate.

"I won't," their attacker said, holding her sword aloft, "let you beat me the same way twice. I have telekinesis now, as well."

"Beat this!" Psyche yelled, holding the first two fingers of her right hand to her temple. The woman collapsed to her knees with a cry of pain, grabbing at her head with both hands, but still managing to maintain her grip on her sword.

Sphere and Graviton fell, gasping, to the ground. Graviton immediately reached out toward the blonde woman, who flew into the air. She sailed into the distance, impacting the ground on the side of a mountain in the distance, in the direction of Red Rock Canyon.

"Damn it!" Pyre exclaimed, whirling to face Graviton. "We need to capture her!" He sighed, and tried to will the frustration out of his voice. Pointing in the direction she'd gone, he said, "Let's go find where she landed." He launched himself into the sky, and the others quickly began to follow suit.

Versipellis helped Graviton to her feet and asked, "Hell of a first week, huh?" He shifted form, growing a pair of red, dragon-like wings, and took flight with Graviton as they followed the rest of the team.

"Tell me," Graviton began, then coughed, and continued, "why I joined up, again?"

"'Cause you're a masochist?" Versipellis quipped in reply.

"There she is!" Pyre called over the team's earbuds, pointing downward and ahead of them. "Hit her hard! Sphere, hammerhead!" At that command, Sphere took the forward position in the team's formation, and raised a forcefield in front of the group. They dove, and slammed into the woman's position at full force.

And then they kept falling. The rock face collapsed when the force-field struck. They landed deep underground, in a cave of some sort. As the dust settled, they realized that, wherever they were, it wasn't a natural formation in the rock. They picked themselves up from the rubble left behind by their passage, and took in their surroundings. The walls were high, almost three stories tall, and perfectly straight and smooth.

Light poured in from the hole created when they broke through from the surface, but there were also dozens of artificial lights, twenty feet tall and twice as wide, lining the top of the walls, and they emitted a soft light that filled the massive chamber. Doorways led into other areas, concealed in shadow. Three saucer-shaped craft made of a gleaming, seamless metal sat, unpowered and inert, in the room with them.

"What," Sphere began, looking around, "the actual hell."

Bipedal figures that were most certainly not human burst into the room, carrying what most certainly were weapons of some kind. One of them pointed its rifle-like weapon and a screeching noise came from its mouth. Its companions took aim with their weapons as well, and they all opened fire. Energy beams bounced off of a hastily-erected forcefield as Sphere cried out in profane surprise.

"Get to the surface!" Pyre cried out as the team began taking fire from multiple directions. They took flight with Sphere providing cover for their escape. Overhead, the news helicopters hovered, taking in the incredible scene in what was most certainly now a live feed to their respective stations.

"Psyche," Pyre called out, "anything?" He let loose a torrent of flame, incinerating some of the attacking aliens as they continued to fire at the retreating team.

"They're so alien," Psyche began, holding her hand to her temple once more. "They want to kill us all."

"No kidding," Sphere said as energy weapons fire continued to ricochet off of his forcefields. "We just wrecked their roof," he quipped.

"No," Psyche corrected. "Humans. *Every* human."

The alien weapons fire intensified as more of them joined the group beneath the opening in the side of the mountain. Beams of energy shot skyward, barely missing a Huey near Pyre.

"Protect the civilians!" he called, and a moment later energy beams deflected away from a forcefield erected beneath another of the news helicopters.

As the team led the helicopters to safety, Graviton and Versipellis boarded the Huey, taking a seat so they could rest.

"What the hell was that?" Sphere asked, glancing behind them.

"The aliens you didn't believe were real," Pyre replied, flying at the point of their formation as they made their way back toward Las Vegas. Their earbuds served not only as a means of communication with police dispatch and their headquarters, but also with one another when they were separated or flying, as they were now, when distance and wind noise would have otherwise made it impossible to speak to each other.

Graviton looked out from the door of the Huey. "Anyone see where the crazy chick disappeared to?" she asked.

"West," Psyche replied, the wind blowing her hair into her face. "Into the desert."

"She'll be back," Pyre said. "We'll worry about her later." He paused as a pair of fighter jets, scrambled from nearby Nellis Air Force Base, streaked past, heading to the location of the formerly hidden alien base. Seconds later, they could hear the unmistakable sound of high explosives detonating. "We've got bigger problems right now."

—$—

Two days later, the news networks and social media were still buzzing with speculation about what had happened in the desert outside Las Vegas. The team, dressed in regular clothes, was now gathered at a table in the briefing room that Strongman had set up during his tenure as the team's trainer the previous month. At the head of the table stood two government agents, dressed in business attire: a tall, dark-haired man and a shorter, auburn-haired woman, they waited patiently as the young heroes took their seats.

"I'm Agent Cullsy," the woman said after everyone was settled, "from the Department of Superhuman Affairs. This is my partner, Agent Rudlem."

"Until the President gives his press conference this afternoon," Rudlem said, "what we're about to discuss is classified. Even *he* didn't know about it until yesterday."

Cullsy looked at John, who was seated near the agents' position at the head of the table, and sighed. "So, let me get this straight" she began. "A time traveler took you on a tour of history, and showed you an alien invasion in our future."

"Next month," John replied, "and it's not just her. That woman we fought the other day said that she could see the future, and it scared the crap out of her. She called it an apocalypse."

"We're aware of her," Rudlem replied. "Emily Robinson, twenty-two years old, *aka* Siphon, given her ability to absorb other superhumans' powers."

Cullsy clicked a button on a remote control device in her hand, and the image on the screen behind her changed from the seal of the Department of Superhuman Affairs to an image of the aliens taken by the news helicopter crews.

"We call this species Saurians," she began. "Most of what we know about them comes from one of their ships that was brought down in a freak electrical storm in Ro—"

"Roswell," John interrupted. "In 1947. I was there."

"So you say," Cullsy said, unconvinced. She clicked the button again, and the image changed to a grainy, black-and-white photograph of an alien—a Saurian—lying on an examination table, medical equipment from the 1940s visible around it. "Autopsies on the bodies inside," she continued, "showed striking similarities to dinosaurs. Later, DNA tests corroborated the link. In short, they *are* dinosaurs."

"The Yucatan!" John exclaimed. "That village I saw, right before the asteroid hit. That must be why she showed it to me! That was *them!*"

"Which would seem to corroborate your time travel story," Rudlem said.

"For *some* of us," Cullsy interjected.

"How else could he know that detail?" Rudlem asked her.

"There could be a leak somewhere," Cullsy countered. "It's not unheard of. Don't even get me started about Lazar."

"I still don't understand a few things," John interrupted. "How did they get to Mars? And why wait until now to attack?"

"That's classified," Cullsy said immediately.

"They know about this species already," Rudlem noted.

"There are *more* aliens?" Kevin asked, floored.

"We didn't say that," Cullsy quickly denied.

"The Saurians I saw," Pyre said, "sixty-five million years ago looked like they were still in the stone age. They were building huts out of mud and some kind of glass. There's no way they could have gotten to Mars without help."

"But," Dani interrupted, "I thought Mars was uninhabitable."

"It is *now*," Rudlem replied.

"The Saurians ruined their environment somehow," John explained. "That's why they want Earth."

"We've," Rudlem began, choosing his words carefully, "interviewed the few Saurians we've managed to capture. They went into a dark age for millennia after they were transplanted to Mars."

"Earth became a legend to them," Cullsy added.

"Their history and technology developed in fits and starts," Rudlem explained, "much like our own, but they had millions of years of wars that sent them back to the beginning several times over. They finally developed spaceflight about two hundred years ago."

"There was a disaster of some kind," Cullsy added, "about a century ago. Percival Lowell saw it when he was observing Mars through his telescope at the time, but no one know what they were seeing. Thick clouds covered the planet for years. What Lowell had thought was seasonal plant growth cycles just... stopped."

"The pillars of smoke," John said. "I don't know what they were, but they were killing everything. It was worse than the pollution in nineteenth-century London. I could barely breathe."

"They'd already visited Earth a few decades earlier," Rudlem said.

"London," John added. "I was there."

Rudlem nodded and continued, "They knew the legends were true: Earth was their ancestral homeworld, and it could support life."

"But now it was overrun," Cullsy said. "By us."

"They debated for decades," Rudlem continued. "Try to find a peace with us, or conquer us. Every time they came," he shook his head, "we attacked them. They decided it was impossible to live with us, so they decided to kill us, but to find a way to do it without destroying the environment here like they did on Mars."

"They began a clandestine program," Cullsy said, continuing the narrative as the images changed to one of a flying saucer buried under the rubble from the encounter two days earlier, "to undermine our social and technological structures, hoping to foment enough chaos and strife that we might kill ourselves off, solving their problem for them."

"They also began researching bioweapons," Rudlem added. "We've tentatively connected the 1917 Influenza Pandemic to them. We believe this bioweapon research program is the source of the alien abduction phenomenon: abducting test subjects to find more efficient ways to kill us without killing the rest of the life on the planet." He paused, then added, "We also believe that this experimentation on humans led to the unexpected, spontaneous appearance of superpowered capabilities in humans."

The silence as Rudlem's words sunk in was broken a moment later by Kevin, whose response, while vulgar, was a sentiment nevertheless shared by everyone present.

Chapter Twelve

Sentinel leaped back, avoiding the sword as its blade sliced through the air where he had been standing a moment earlier. At the other end of the blade, an enraged blonde woman ranted about how she planned to kill him and take his powers for herself.

Costume aside, Sentinel wasn't just a superhero. He was the official hero of the city of Los Angeles, and a member of the Los Angeles Police Department. When a call came in that involved a superhuman belligerent, he or a member of his team of super-cops were a part of the response. Today, that response was to a call about a psychotic white woman with a sword targeting a Hispanic man in a hardscrabble neighborhood in the shadow of downtown Los Angeles.

By the time Sentinel arrived on the scene with backup from the SWAT team, the young man in question lay dead in the street, and the woman was attacking the victim's associates—all heavily armed, with weapons that were proving entirely useless against her.

This was, sadly, far from Sentinel's first fight, as he had served as a member of Team Liberty, the U.S. military's elite superhuman special forces task force that drew its members from every branch. After his mandatory enlistment had ended, he chose to serve as a police officer in his hometown.

A blurred form zipped past him, stopping next to a young woman on the corner across the street. Now that he wasn't moving at superspeed, Sentinel could see a young man in an oversized t-shirt and shorts, with a bandana covering his hair and large goggles obscuring his face. Dark black hairs jutted from his chin, highlighting his adolescence. The kid wasn't registered, and was taking pains to conceal his identity. Technically, he was breaking the law by acting as a vigilante, but Sentinel wasn't going to push the matter while the kid was helping to evacuate civilians from the area.

"Speedfreak," Sentinel called as he dodged blows from Siphon, throwing a few of his own that failed to connect as well, "status on the civilian evac?"

"Got the last one now, Sentinel!" the kid yelled back before grabbing the young woman by the wrist and zipping away to safety in another blur of motion.

Sentinel found an opening and leaped onto Siphon's back. He wrapped his arms around her shoulders and locked his fingers behind her neck in a full nelson hold. Before she could wrest herself free, Sentinel called to his SWAT support team.

"Tranquilizers!" Sentinel ordered. "Now!" An instant later, three tranquilizer darts struck Siphon's chest while Sentinel held her in place for the sharpshooters to do their job more effectively.

The darts bounced off, landing on the ground at their feet with light, metallic clinks as the aluminum struck the pavement, the needle tips bent sideways. Sentinel looked at the useless darts in surprise as Siphon chuckled.

"That gangbanger I put down?" she began, using her telekinesis to push Sentinel off of her back, where he began to hover, suspended in midair. "Invulnerability. Useless against telekinetically squeezing his carotid artery." Sentinel began to choke as an invisible hand began squeezing his own throat. He, too, was invulnerable, as well as superstrong, and he possessed the ability to fly. None of which protected him from a telekinetic attack like this.

"This will be over soon," Siphon said as she began to casually walk away from him. He hung helplessly in midair, and clutched uselessly at his throat, his legs pistoning beneath him. "I'll put your powers to good use."

"Gas," Sentinel managed to gasp, loudly enough for the earbud embedded in the cowl of his costume to pick up, "her!"

Another member of the SWAT team quickly pulled what looked like a smoke grenade from his belt, though it was labeled instead "Gas, Nerve, Dampening" in large, blocky letters. He pulled the pin and smoke began to erupt from the top of the canister, then hurled the grenade toward Siphon. Halfway through its arc toward her, she launched herself into the sky, safely away from the area. Sentinel fell to the ground, and the canister, smoke still billowing from its opening, clattered to the ground next to him.

"Damn it!" Sentinel cursed amid a coughing fit as he started breathing once again, the air thick with the dampening gas. Normally he would take flight and pursue Siphon, but now he was grounded for the next couple of hours, until the effects of the gas could wear off. He sat on the nearby curb and watched as Siphon receded into the distance.

As his coughing fit began to subside, Sentinel spoke into the microphone pickup on his earbud. "Dispatch," he began, "suspect is in flight, heading southeast. I've been hit with dampening gas and cannot pursue."

"Copy, Sentinel," the voice of the dispatcher said over the earbud. "Aerial units have been advised." A moment later, a pair of helicopters with LAPD painted across their bottoms streaked overhead, heading southeast at a rapid clip. One of the SWAT officers walked up to him, clad in heavy body armor, his AR-15 rifle held at a relaxed, but ready, position.

"Situation?" Sentinel asked as the young man stepped over to him.

"One fatality," the officer reported. "Six injured. The speedster got the crowd out in time, sir."

"Glad he was in the area, then," Sentinel replied, though as fast as the kid could move, anywhere in the city could potentially be considered as "in the area." As if on cue, Speedfreak zipped up next to him, now that the cloud of gas had dissipated.

"You a'ight?" Speedfreak asked, in what sounded to Sentinel like an affected accent, rather than his actual speech pattern. The kid was clever, he noted.

"My powers will be back in an hour or so," Sentinel replied, rubbing his head. The gas was giving him a mild headache as well, which was a common side-effect. He hoped that his nose wouldn't start running; that wouldn't be very dignified once the news cameras got there. "Thanks for the help, kid," Sentinel continued. He looked up at the young, would-be hero and flashed a knowing grin. "Have you reconsidered my offer?" He knew the answer already, but he had to ask.

Predictably, the kid stepped back and threw his hands up in front of him, almost defensively. "Uh-uh," he replied. "I ain't signin' up with da man."

"I might," Sentinel countered, trying to hide the amusement in his voice, "have to arrest you, then. Vigilantism's illegal, after all."

"It ain't like that, man," Speedfreak replied. "I'm just a," he paused for a heartbeat, and Sentinel could hear the subtle change in his voice as he continued, "concerned citizen."

"Offer's still on the table, kid," Sentinel replied as he stood up from the curb and brushed the legs of his costume. The suits upstairs called it a uniform, but as far as Sentinel was concerned, it was a costume: a dark blue bodysuit with light blue arms ending in dark blue gloves, topped with a dark blue cowl that left only his eyes and mouth exposed. The belt featured a stylized "S" in a circle on the buckle, and he was still fighting with his superiors to at least let him wear a badge on the belt; he was still a cop, after all.

"We could use your help more often," Sentinel continued. Speedfreak was *listening*, at least. "Think about it!" he admonished.

Speedfreak nodded, then flashed a two-fingered mock salute at Sentinel. In a blur of motion, he was gone. Moments later, an ambulance pulled around the corner, followed by a pair of news vans from two of the local news stations.

Showtime, Sentinel thought, mocking himself for the next role that his position required of him: public relations.

— § —

Speedfreak zipped back into normal time in his bedroom in East Los Angeles. Ever since his superspeed powers had first appeared a few months earlier, he'd been struggling to understand how they worked. It seemed to him that, rather than him moving fast, the rest of the world seemed to slow to a crawl. Maybe it was semantic, maybe he created a bubble of accelerated time around himself; he wasn't sure how it worked, exactly, but he didn't seem to be affected by friction from the air when he ran, nor were the people he took to safety earlier.

Using his speed once again, he changed back into his regular clothes, and hid his costume deep in his closet. Moments later, his bedroom door opened, and an older woman entered the bedroom. She had streaks of gray in her long black hair, and wrinkles creased the corners of her eyes and mouth.

"There you are, *mijo*," the woman said. "I've been looking for you."

"I just got back home, *abuela*," he said. "Is everything all right?"

"*Sí, sí*," the woman, his grandmother, replied. "Dinner is almost ready."

"Great," he said, smiling. "I'm starving."

His grandmother shook her head and laughed. "Boys," she said. "Always so hungry. Where do you put it, Alejandro?" She pinched his arm. "As much as you eat, you are so thin."

"I get a lot of exercise, *abuela*,"he replied.

She studied him through narrowed eyes for a moment, then turned and walked out of the room. "Come to dinner, *mijo*." Following his grandmother, he found his mother setting the table, while his father watched the news on the television in the living room, and his younger siblings played with their toys on the living room carpet. While his siblings were too young to understand or care about the news, it caused his stomach to churn in worry and anticipation.

"The Supreme Court," the news anchor said on the screen, "has agreed to hear arguments against President Obama's executive actions on immigration. The issue of the DREAM Act has gained significant attention in recent months, as the presidential election—"

"Is everything all right, Alejandro?" his mother asked, noticing that he was standing completely still in the space between the living room and the dining room in the family's apartment.

"Yeah," he said with a sigh. "Just watching the news."

His mother nodded. "There are things you can control," she said, "and things you can't. That is something that you can't control. Your father and I brought you here for a better life, but we couldn't control the system that changed the rules every time we tried to come, and made it so hard to do it the way they said they wanted. You have to have faith that things will work out in the end."

Alejandro nodded. His parents, Maribel and Jose Garcia, had come to America when he was a baby, but he only learned that they had crossed the border illegally less than a year ago, not long before his powers first appeared. The DREAM Act gave him hope that he could achieve the citizenship status he'd grown up thinking that he already had, in the only country he'd ever known as his home, but now that was being called into question during this election. It made him feel so powerless, and he feared for his family's future.

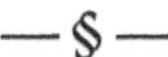

The command center was abuzz with activity. Technicians and tactical specialists flitted from station to station as they went about their duties. Ever since the outpost in Nevada was revealed on live television almost two weeks earlier, operations had increased to an almost frenetic tempo.

At the heart of it all, a large, circular table was set aside that provided a strategic overview for the higher-ups who oversaw global operations. Two figures stood side-by-side at the table. A light shone from the table's center, projecting an enormous holographic representation of the planet several feet above the table's surface. It rotated slowly, and labels extended from multiple points across the globe, indicating major cities on every inhabited continent.

Beside the holographic display table, the two Saurians stood silently, reviewing the material being displayed for them. Though illegible to any but the best-trained human eyes, the labels hovering above the gently rotating globe relayed a great deal of data: the name of each location, a number grading that location's threat assessment value, and a date and time stamp.

The unexpected revelation of the advanced reconnaissance forces on Earth to the general human population was distressing. Their plan had been for a much longer-term extermination of the humans, in a way that would preserve the planet and its resources to the greatest extent possible. Contingency plans had been drawn up, to be certain, but the outcome of a direct assault on humanity had always been a risky proposition at best.

The projections displayed on the globe seemed hopelessly optimistic to Strike Leader Kssarr. He had encountered humans before, and knew how effective they could be in combat. He shook his head and looked to his companion, Strike Leader Visz.

"We're not ready," he said in the gutteral, sibilant Saurian language.

"It doesn't matter," Visz replied. "We're out of time."

CHAPTER THIRTEEN

Don Bryton sipped water from the drinking tube within the helmet of his spacesuit. He had been in the suit for more than an hour, and that was after several hours of traveling across the lunar surface, first in a suborbital hopper, and then in a lunar rover. He and the other half-dozen men in his team were far beyond explored territory on the moon, and were nearly on the opposite side of the globe from their home at Armstrong Colony in the Sea of Tranquility.

They had been sent to investigate an "anomalous energy reading" that just happened to be in the same general direction that the flying saucer that Lieber and King had spotted a month ago had been flying toward. Aliens had been confirmed on live television a few weeks ago, and now they'd been sent out to check out an energy surge halfway around the moon. As soon as the structure came into view, they stopped the rover and parked it in the shadow behind a ridge, where it was unlikely to be noticed. They then made the rest of the trip on foot, sticking to the shadows as much as possible.

"That's an impressive-looking energy reading," Don muttered as he peered over the ridge that the group was hiding behind before making the final push toward the structure that now towered over them. It was made of a gleaming, silvery metal, just like the ship that Lieber and King had seen, and it was about twenty stories tall. Pillars and spires made up of triangles and curves projected into the sky, pointing into the darkness of space. The center of the mass of shapes was almost pyramidal.

"Over there," another member of the group, Lee McDuffie, said, pointing toward a shadowed area near the base of the structure. "That looks like an airlock." Although everyone's spacesuits were more or less identical, each person had a different colored stripe on their arms and waist, to help them tell each other apart at a glance. McDuffie wore red, and he had taken *de facto* command of the scouting party. The well-armed scouting party, as everyone carried a rifle that had been designed for use in space, save for Don himself.

In Don's case, his suit had more than just green stripes to differentiate him from the others. His suit also had a unique pair of gauntlets made of a brass-colored metal that had been created for him to be able to use his powers in the vacuum of space. He had been working for the past two months as part of the construction teams building an expansion of the colony, and his powers had been incredibly helpful in clearing huge sections of rock to make way for the new facilities. The metal gauntlets on his suit were linked to a small supply of reactant gases, which could be bled into the space around his hands, and he could then use his powers to ignite those gases into a highly-charged plasma. The supply of reactant gases was limited, of course, so he had switches built into the gloves that controlled the gas flow.

The half-dozen humans quickly moved across the lunar surface from their place of concealment to the presumed airlock, hoping that they had not been seen. They had seen footage of these aliens in Nevada—where Don's half-brother David Brown, who was a superhero called Nucleus, had unexpectedly exposed an alien invasion force on live television with the rest of his superhero team, the Protectorate—and if that was any indication of what they were about to encounter, they were in a very precarious position.

Two days after the Protectorate's encounter made the news, President Obama went on television and confirmed that these aliens had been coming to earth for at least 150 years, and their intentions were hostile. Humanity had managed to capture a few of them and some of their ships, and that had helped in understanding their technology, and it also provided a boost to human technology as their devices were reverse-engineered.

The scouting party entered the airlock—McDuffie had been correct—and waited as the atmosphere cycled in and stabilized. Just like their own airlocks, jets of compressed air not only filled the chamber with breathable gases, but also sprayed them down with the gases to dislodge any loose regolith dust from their suits. The lunar surface had no water or atmosphere to speak of, so there was no erosion as a result. The bits of rock and dust had razor-sharp edges that would have been worn down to smooth surfaces on Earth, and breathing that dust in could cause significant lung damage.

McDuffie checked the computer display on the wrist of his suit. A series of graphs and numbers scrolled across the display, and an animated cartoon character popped up, then flashed a thumbs-up. The word "NOMINAL" blinked on the top half of the display, and a word balloon appeared above the cartoon character that said, "Good to go!"

"I'm reading a breathable atmosphere in here," McDuffie said. He reached up and removed his helmet. He breathed tentatively, held it for a moment, then relaxed slightly as he exhaled. "Helmets off," he said, "but keep them handy... just in case."

Everyone attached their helmets to the side of their belts. The suits had been designed for this; the belts had a series of carabiner clips to attach tools and other devices, and the helmets had a loop built into them that allowed them to be clipped onto the belt for easy carry. If you were working in an area where you needed your suit, but were able to take off the helmet, yet still needed to wear the rest of the suit, it followed that you might find yourself in a situation where you would need to put that helmet back on in a hurry. Fortunately, hard experience through both testing and accidents had shown that a person could survive exposure to vacuum for up to about two minutes, though the longer the exposure, the greater the damage from oxygen deprivation and radiation exposure.

Everyone kept their weapons ready, including Don, who kept a charge of plasma around his fists as they slowly made their way from the airlock and into the rest of the facility. It was eerie how similar the structure was to their own base, though Don supposed that one hallway would ultimately look a lot like another. It didn't take long before they were spotted.

As they rounded a corner, an alien in some kind of body armor whipped its head in their direction, and a second later let out a screeching sound that Don supposed must have been something like "Intruders!" or "Humans!" or something along those lines. An instant later, a dozen aliens in similar attire, all of which were holding rifle-like weapons of some sort, turned and ran in their direction. Some started shooting.

Don shot back. He took out a couple of them, but there were so many, it didn't seem to have any effect on them. They just kept coming. McDuffie's head snapped back as he took aim with his own rifle, and he slumped to the ground. Blood pooled from a wound between his eyes, which were staring in wide-eyed, unblinking shock.

As much as he hated his time in the Marine Corps, brief as it was, Don's training kicked in. He let loose a torrent of plasma, creating a wall of energy that set several of the attacking Saurians on fire. He and another member of the team grabbed McDuffie by the shoulders and dragged him as they retreated toward the airlock.

— § —

"There were too many of them," Don said on the video screen. He had sent a message to his estranged sibling on Earth, and now it was being replayed for the entire team in the briefing room. "We barely got out of there, and we took heavy losses." He paused, then leaned into the camera. "They're here. There's thousands of them, maybe more. If your team can get over here, we need your help."

"David received this message an hour ago," Pyre said, leaning forward in his chair at the large table in the briefing room of the Protectorate's headquarters in Las Vegas. "We've already been in contact with the Department of Superhuman Affairs and we've been cleared to fly directly to Edwards Air Force Base in California, where a spaceship is already prepped and waiting on the pad, ready to take us to the moon." He looked at everyone at the table, making eye contact with every member of his team, before continuing, "We leave in fifteen minutes. Grab your go bags and meet up on the roof." Everyone blinked and stared at him, dumbfounded, for a moment. As his words sunk in, they stood and made their way to the exit.

"This is it," Sphere began. "The invasion you saw. It's happening, isn't it?"

Pyre looked at his friend. Until last month, Sphere hadn't even be-lieved his story, but then they saw the aliens up close and personal. Except they weren't really aliens, Pyre now knew. These Saurians, as the government called them, were actually descended from intelligent dinosaurs that had somehow been transplanted to Mars before the comet wiped them all out. Now that they'd ruined their adopted planet, they wanted Earth back, and were willing to wipe out every living person to get it.

"Looks like it," Pyre admitted. He clapped Sphere on the shoulder. "Go get your stuff. The DSA's got a plane waiting for us at McCarran."

Sphere left the briefing room, and Pyre followed after him a moment later. Each member of the team had their own suite of rooms one floor down. The facility had been converted from the upper floors of the Chambers Casino and Resort, and their rooms were formerly luxury suites in the hotel. Pyre went to his suite, and pulled a duffel bag from the closet in the bedroom.

After he and the others had graduated from high school the week before, Pyre had effectively moved in, and had been staying here full time. He looked around at his rooms, and turned to leave, only to find his father waiting at the door.

"I wanted to catch you before you left," Max Chambers said. He was wearing his usual business suit and tie, although he had apparently left the suit jacket in his office. He had his hands in his pockets, which was unusual for him. He reached up and adjusted his glasses, then began to play with the pocket of his pants.

He's worried, Pyre realized, *and trying not to show it.* Pyre set his bag down and wrapped his arms around his father.

"I'll be okay, dad," he reassured the older man.

Max patted Pyre on the back, his arms wrapped around his son. "Can't blame me for worrying," he admitted.

"I'll be fine," Pyre reiterated. "This is my job now." Max gave him an odd look, but said nothing. The two walked together in silence to the roof, where the rest of the team was gathering.

Once everyone was present, they launched themselves into the air and flew together to McCarran International Airport. It was a short flight, less than four miles, and took only a few minutes. They were met on the tarmac by a DSA representative, and boarded a small government jet. Within minutes, they were airborne once again, and en route to Edwards Air Force Base, about two hundred miles away.

They could have flown on their own, but security concerns from the military meant that clearing a single, government-registered aircraft was easier for their procedures than doing the same for a half-dozen civilian superhumans. Besides, it gave the team time to relax and prepare for their next steps.

After landing, the team was quickly briefed on the procedures for the emergency launch, and loaded into the capsule less than two hours after arriving at Edwards, despite a great deal of grumbling and hand-wringing from the flight surgeons over the irregularity of the situation.

The launch came soon thereafter. Within minutes of liftoff, the young heroes found themselves in space for the first time, and marveled at the view through the windows of the spacecraft.

"This is the captain," a voice said in their earbuds, which had been linked into the spacecraft's communications system. "The moon is at apogee, so travel time will be somewhat longer than usual; the trip will take about three and a half days."

"Oh, hell no," Graviton said. She pushed herself off from the wall and made her way into the cockpit module. "I can speed this up, captain," she said. "Just point us in the right direction." She closed her eyes, taking hold of the co-pilot's seat in front of her. There was a jolt, and the spacecraft leaped forward. The captain's jaw dropped in astonishment as he studied the readouts on his display.

"The speeds you're pushing us at are incredible, Graviton!" he exclaimed. "At this rate, we'll make it to the moon in about twelve *hours!*"

"Can you keep this up for that long?" Pyre asked, floating up into the cockpit module beside her.

"I don't need to," she replied. "Inertia will carry us until I need to slow us down."

"Oh," Pyre replied. "Right. Space."

Graviton chuckled. "I paid attention in my physics class," she replied. "Figured it would come in handy with these powers."

—§—

"Thank you for getting here so quickly," the thirty-something, dark-haired man said as he rose from his desk. "I'm Martin Jefferson, administrator of Armstrong Colony." He reached out and offered his hand, which Pyre took, giving a firm handshake.

"We were told the situation was urgent," Pyre replied. The gravity on the moon was far weaker than he was used to, but, so far at least, he'd managed to avoid embarrassing himself by hitting the ceiling.

"It is," Jefferson replied, breaking the handshake and briefly looking each of his guests in the eye. "I've been authorized to reveal this facility's true purpose to you."

"Its *true* purpose?" Sphere asked.

"They already knew the Saurians were here," Pyre concluded, folding his arms across his chest.

"We suspected," Jefferson admitted. "Strongly. But we couldn't find their base's location until a few days ago. You already know how our scouting mission went." He paused, shaking his head in frustration. Collecting his composure, he continued, "Our job here is to find and counter the Saurian threat to Earth, by whatever means necessary."

Pyre nodded. "What do you need us to do?"

Chapter Fourteen

All traffic had ground to a halt on Fifth Street. That in and of itself wasn't unusual in Los Angeles, although rush hour wasn't due to begin for several more hours. Most of the drivers and their passengers had exited their cars, and everyone was staring at the spectacle unfolding in the sky above them.

Sentinel stood near the edge of Pershing Square, located between Fifth and Sixth Streets in downtown Los Angeles. An enormous, saucer-shaped craft made of a gleaming, silvery metal had slowly moved into position to hover over the skyscrapers at the heart of downtown LA.

With a slight disturbance in the air around him, Speedfreak appeared at Sentinel's side. The young man was a teenaged superhuman whose heart was clearly in the right place, but who refused to come forward and register as a licensed superhero, as the law required. Sentinel suspected that the young man's reticence may be related to the political rhetoric regarding immigrants, given the kid's obvious Hispanic background. Whatever his reasons, the kid still needed to register if he wanted to keep being a superhero, and eventually Sentinel would have to force the issue.

"*¡Madre de dios!*" Speedfreak breathed. Sentinel glanced at the young, would-be hero. For once, he was absolutely still. His mouth hung agape, the wispy black hairs on his chin swaying in the light breeze, while large goggles concealed his eyes and obscured the shape of his face, and a bandana covered his hair.

"You can say that again, kid," Sentinel agreed quietly.

A tearing sound and a flash of light caught his eye. In the distance, Sentinel noticed two people who hadn't been there moments earlier. One of them was a red-haired woman in a gray jacket, green shirt, and blue jeans, whom he didn't recognize. The other person, however, he knew very well.

"Pyre?" Sentinel asked, confused. There was no way for them to hear him from this distance, but the question was more for himself than for them. He began to jog toward Pyre and the woman. What were they doing in LA? Did they know this UFO was going to show up? How could they have known that?

"There's more that you need to see," the woman said as Sentinel drew closer. What Sentinel could only describe as a rip in the sky appeared. Inside, it was a mass of roiling energy and red clouds. As the woman stepped through and vanished, Pyre followed.

"Pyre!" Sentinel called. "*John!*" But as soon as the words left his mouth, Pyre vanished as well. The rift in the air sealed itself, then disappeared as if it had never been there.

"Dude!" Speedfreak exclaimed as he zipped up to stand beside Sentinel once again. "They just *vanished!*"

Screams drew Sentinel's attention back to the congested street nearby, and pointed fingers drew it again to the alien spacecraft hovering over the city. A large hatch on the underside of the craft was cycling open, revealing a cavernous, seemingly empty chamber at the heart of the spacecraft. As the hatch slowly opened, dozens of smaller, similarly-shaped craft began pouring out of the mothership, and streaked down toward the city below.

"Come on," Sentinel said. "We've got other things to worry about."

— § —

The airlock finished cycling, and a dozen people in spacesuits stepped through the now-open doorway, into an empty hallway. The spacesuits were all identical, differentiated only by stripes of color on the upper arms and waists of the suits. One of the people, in a suit marked in red, reached up and removed the helmet, revealing a young face with blond hair: Pyre. Moments later, the others removed their helmets as well, revealing the rest of the Protectorate, Plasmid, and several armed members of Armstrong Colony's paramilitary forces.

"This is too easy," Sphere said as he removed his spacesuit, revealing his uniform underneath. The likelihood of the Saurians exposing the interior of their own base to vacuum seemed extremely unlikely, and the task force had chosen to remove their suits to give themselves greater flexibility and maneuverability while within the facility. "They *have* to know we're here!"

"You're right," Pyre replied. The Saurians had laid an ambush for the last group that had attempted to breach the facility; it stood to reason that they were planning the same tactic once again. He looked to Psyche, whose brow was already furrowed in concentration. "Anything, Psyche?"

Raising a hand to her head as she closed her eyes, to aid in her concentration, Psyche replied, "They're so hard to read." Suddenly, her eyes snapped open in shock. "Oh my God!" she exclaimed. "It's started!"

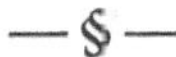

Traffic ground to a halt as the giant Saurian spacecraft hovered over London. The congestion was made worse when panicked drivers leaped out of their cars to run.

The chaos was spreading throughout the city, as evidenced on the Heads-Up Display within Antonia Thatcher's helmet. Known publicly as the Iron Lady, Thatcher was one of the United Kingdom's premiere heroes, and wore a full-body suit of powered armor of her own invention.

As she made her way against the flow of panicked humanity, she walked as calmly as she could manage *toward* the giant flying saucer. She could have flown, certainly, but the Iron Lady was trying to calm the crowd by projecting an air of confidence. The crowd parted to provide her with a path, at least, but they didn't seem any calmer.

"Heading your way, boss," the voice of a young woman called out through the headphones mounted in the Iron Lady's helmet. A moment later, another figure clad in in powered armor streaked into view overhead, then landed several feet in front of the Iron Lady.

Where the Iron Lady's armor was shades of gold and silver, the newcomer was decorated in blue and red, and she sported a pair of enormous, butterfly-like wings mounted to the back of her suit.

"Blue's meeting us at Big Ben," the newcomer said without preamble. The Iron Lady nodded. This was her sidekick—a term the younger woman hated, which only prompted her to use it more—Pixie Pristine. When she wasn't acting as a superhero—and a pain in the Iron Lady's backside—Pixie Pristine was better known to the world as Hannah Wilson, pop music sensation.

Far smarter than her bubbly public persona would lead one to believe, she had deduced the Iron Lady's identity through a series of well-placed questions and social engagements. Approaching Thatcher in her private identity, she begged the older woman to take her on as a partner. Eventually, Thatcher relented, and the odd couple of British herodom was born.

Activating their suits' jet boots, they launched into the sky. The Iron Lady's suit did not have wings—something Pixie Pristine had specifically requested. Instead, she maneuvered with a system of reaction thrusters positioned throughout the suit.

About a block away from their destination, they landed. They could see Royal Blue conferring with a group of officers from the Royal Army and from the local police, and the giant spaceship hung ominously overhead. Royal Blue was Daniel Hetherington, a former SAS soldier with superstrength, as well as enhanced speed and hearing, who, after leaving the Royal Army, had been recruited to serve as the face of the Royal Guard, Britain's premiere team of superheroes, of which the Iron Lady and Pixie Pristine were also members. Walking the rest of the way toward the group of heroes, soldiers, and police, Pixie Pristine began talking, as usual, about virtually anything that came to mind.

"Maybe," she began, "this will get people to talk about something besides Harambe." She laughed at her own joke; clearly, she was extremely nervous and trying—and failing—not to show it.

The Iron Lady took the bait. "People got obsessed with Harambe even after the aliens were on TV last month. The Internet has the attention span of a goldfish."

A sound of metal gears moving caught their attention. Looking up, they could see a circular hatch beginning to iris open at the bottom of the Saurian vessel. The Iron Lady looked back at Pixie Pristine, and pointed to the group of military officers, police, and other superheroes ahead of them.

"We need to get over there now!"

—§—

As the smaller Saurian ships poured out from the mothership that hovered over Washington, DC, soldiers readied for the inevitable conflict. Some of them had super powers, and many of them did not. Nervous energy surged through all of their veins. Tanks took aim, waiting for the order to open fire. Sergeants barked orders, passed down through their chain of command. Much higher up that chain, senior military leadership met in the situation room deep within the Pentagon.

"We're getting reports from around the globe," one of the generals said. He wore the blue uniform of the United States Air Force, and the brushed chrome name tag on his jacket's right breast said that he was General Mark Welsh, the Chief of Staff of the Air Force. His graying hair was receding, but while it was kept in a short, neat style, it was not as short as his Army or Marine counterparts. "These motherships are appearing over major cities and national capitols worldwide. The count now stands at forty-seven."

"Three confirmed in the U.S.," added General Frank Grass, the Chief of the National Guard Bureau. "Los Angeles, New York City, and Washington, DC. Standby forces are at the ready."

"The president is contacting the embassies," began General Joseph Dunford, the Chairman of the Joint Chiefs of Staff, straightening the olive drab jacket of his Marine Corps uniform, "and extending an offer of aid. Our forces overseas can coordinate with local governments for mutual defense." Heads nodded around the table and an aide stepped away, furiously taking notes.

"The Protectorate is already on the moon," General Welsh added. "They left as soon as we got word about the Saurian base that was discovered on the far side."

"That was less than two days ago," the Vice Chairman, Air Force General Paul Selva, remarked in surprise. "How did they get there already? They should still be only halfway there!"

"One of their members," Welsh replied, "can manipulate gravitational fields. She got them there in twelve hours." Eyes widened and someone whistled. "They're arriving on site at the Saurian base with Armstrong's strike team as we speak."

"Nothing more we can do about the moon," Dunford interjected. "It would take days to send additional forces there. Let's focus our attention closer to home. Team Liberty is headquartered out of Fort Wadsworth; we'll have them focus on the New York mothership. What assets do we have in place for LA and DC?"

—§—

"You're insane," Karl Brown said as his boyfriend, Walter Campbell, tugged at the jacket he had pulled from the closet, adjusting it to fit over his shoulders more comfortably.

"I have to do something," Walter said as he grabbed a large, webbed belt laden with utility pouches, and snapped it into place around his waist.

"Like get yourself killed?" Karl retorted.

"I've got super powers," Walter replied. "I can help."

"Help how?" Karl asked. "You gonna *grow* something at 'em, *Leafmaster?*"

Walter sighed. He put his hands on Karl's shoulders and looked into his eyes.

"I know you're worried," Walter said. "I am, too. But I can't just sit here when I know that I can help." He leaned forward and kissed Karl, his arms wrapping around the man he loved. They embraced for several seconds before Walter pulled away.

"I'll be careful," Walter said.

"You'd better," Karl replied.

"And I'll be back," Walter said.

"You'd better," Karl repeated, and Walter chuckled.

"I love you," Walter said.

"You'd better," Karl said once again.

Chapter Fifteen

The Protectorate made their way through the corridor in the Saurian base. Their path was far from unobstructed, however, as hundreds of Saurian soldiers had attempted to stop their progress. The base was clearly designed as a command and control hub for the invasion effort, which supported the intelligence analysis that had been provided to the team during their trip from Earth to the moon. Given the limitations of light-speed communications, transmissions between Earth and Mars could take up to 24 minutes each way, depending on where the planets were in their orbits, so having a command center closer to Earth would be an advantage. By comparison, the moon's communications delay of about two-and-a-half seconds was negligible.

With that in mind, while the rest of the world fought off the Saurians' front-line attacks, the Protectorate was sent to lead what forces that Armstrong Colony could muster against the Saurian base on the far side of the moon. If they could find a way to cut those Earthbound forces off from their command network, it would go a long way to helping ensure victory against the Saurian invaders. Unfortunately, once inside the base, they had no idea where that command and control facility might be located. With no other guide, they just continued deeper into the base, hoping to stumble onto their target while causing enough mayhem and destruction in the process to further distract the Saurian leadership.

The team made slow progress, but it was progress nonetheless, and they fought for every step. Pyre led the charge, and he, Nucleus, and Plasmid provided long-range fire against the Saurians. Versipellis had bulked up with muscle mass beneath his chitinous armor, and his clawed hands ripped through the Saurian forces as the team advanced. Sphere provided cover in the form of a forcefield around himself, Psyche, and Graviton, and the two young women battered the oncoming Saurians with telekinesis and gravitational waves, keeping them off-balance against the rest of the team's attacks. The strike team that had accompanied them from Armstrong followed closely behind them, fighting off the attacking Saurians with the rifles, handguns, and even knives that they had brought along for the battle.

Without clear directions, Pyre chose to press the attack to whichever direction the Saurians were defending the fiercest. As they made their way through the alien-yet-familiar corridors, the number of defenders and the intensity of the fighting only increased, and the corridors themselves all seemed to be heading toward a central location. Pyre hoped that meant that he was going the right way, and that the Saurian leaders hadn't duped him with a feint.

— § —

"Clear the area!" Sentinel yelled as he launched himself skyward. He rocketed toward the Saurian fighter craft, fists forward, as they began to descend from the mothership hovering over downtown Los Angeles. Speedfreak watched, awed, for a moment as Sentinel climbed into the sky.

But only for a moment. He shook his head, bringing himself back to the terrifying reality around him. The aliens were here, and they were invading.

The world around him slowed to a crawl as he willed himself into superspeed. He jogged over to the nearest person. She was a young woman, probably in her mid-twenties, with blonde hair and fair skin. Speedfreak paused a moment, which was less than a nanosecond to the rest of the world, and took a breath.

Having readied himself for the task that was to come, which happened every time he did this, he took the first step. Literally, in fact, as he approached the woman. He took hold of her wrist, and she suddenly began to move.

"What the hell?" she practically screamed. "Where did you—?" She stopped, realizing he was holding her forearm. "Hey! Let go, you little creep!"

"Calm down!" Speedfreak interrupted. "We're at superspeed, but only as long as I'm touching you. I need to get everyone here to safety." The young woman tried to wrest her arm away, but Speedfreak's grip was practiced and strong.

"Let me go!" she repeated, angrily. "Who the f—"

"We don't have time for this," Speedfreak interrupted, "even at superspeed! Look! The aliens are attacking *right now!*" He pointed, and the young woman followed his gesture. Alien spacecraft were floating, suspended in midair, as they left their docks within the mothership. A passenger jet was visible in the distance, a gnat frozen in place on its approach to Los Angeles International Airport, several miles away near the coast. Closer to them, Sentinel hovered, his fists forward like a battering ram pointed straight at the closest alien ship. Her jaw dropped.

"I can't just pick you up and run off," Speedfreak explained. "My powers don't work like that, and even if they did, I don't have the strength or the stamina to do that with everyone here." He waved his arm, indicating the crowd surrounding them. "Walk with me, and I'll get you somewhere safe, because I think a bunch of wrecked spaceships are about to come down *right here.*"

Blinking in sudden, shocked understanding, the young woman followed as Speedfreak led her on a brisk walk out of the area. Several subjective minutes—and a fraction of a second in real time—later, he let go of her arm, and she froze once more.

Speedfreak turned, and began to jog back to Pershing Square. Not for the first time, he was beginning to wonder if a bicycle—or even a motorcycle—would still work at superspeed, because all of this running was exhausting.

—§—

Night had begun to fall in London, and the area around Big Ben's clock tower was even darker than usual thanks to the shadow of the enormous alien mothership hovering overhead. None of that mattered to the Iron Lady, however, as her suit's optical sensors automatically compensated for low-light conditions.

She landed several yards from Royal Blue's left and was joined a moment later by Pixie Pristine. Opposite her, on Royal Blue's right, another figure landed, also having flown in from elsewhere in the city. He was large, powerfully built, and had graying hair and a close-cropped gray beard. He wore a white bodysuit with a Union Jack across his chest, with blue gloves and boots, and a red cape with gold trim flowed behind him as he landed.

"Oh, bloody perfect," a dark-haired man in a long, dark coat muttered nearby as he took a drag off of his cigarette, "the Wanker's here." His companions, a hulking brute of a man and a petite woman with enormous, feathered wings sprouting from her back, laughed quietly. While the Iron Lady agreed that Lord Albion was not always the most pleasant person to be around, he was also a member of her team and deserved respect.

"Have a care," she said, approaching the trio. "And who might you be?"

"MI5," the man in the long coat said, eyeing her warily. "Special operations. I'm called Gaffer. This lot is Bloke," he indicated the wall of muscle to his right with a nod, then nodded at the winged woman, "and Bird. They call us the Bollocks, 'cause we've got enough to take the piss out of you hero types when you step out of line."

"Charmed," the Iron Lady replied, her voice thick with sarcasm. "I hope you're here to help with this situation," she indicated the alien ships, which had begun to disgorge themselves from the mothership overhead. "Or is that beneath you?" Before Gaffer could reply, she turned away and stepped over to Royal Blue and Lord Albion.

"Iron Lady," Royal Blue said in greeting. "I've received word that this is happening worldwide. Dozens of these motherships. It's up to us to stop this lot here before they can destroy London."

—§—

Kenji Tanaka secured himself into his cockpit with a complicated series of belts and harnesses. They were snug, but necessary. He smoothed the form-fitting material of his flight suit with the palms of his hands. Taking a series of calming breaths, he found his center. Opening his eyes, he reached out and retrieved his helmet from atop the control panel in front of him.

Slipping the helmet over his close-cropped, black hair, Kenji secured the straps that would hold the helmet in place. Once he was satisfied that everything was securely fastened, he looked up and flashed a thumbs-up at his crew chief, Chiharu Tsukiyama.

She was a young woman, with flowing black hair and fashionable eyeglasses that drew Kenji's attention to her eyes. Not that her utility suit, a single-piece garment not unlike his flight suit, wasn't extremely flattering on her figure, Kenji noted.

Time and a place, Kenji mentally scolded himself, bringing his focus back to the task at hand. Chiharu nodded and secured the hatch, locking Kenji inside of his cockpit. Monitors blinked on, giving system status reports. He glanced at them all, satisfied with the readings.

"All systems are go," Kenji said in Japanese. "Initiating neural interface." He flipped a series of controls, then pressed a large, red, circular button.

The giant mechanical battlesuit shifted. Its head turned from side to side, then up and down, as if it had suddenly come to life and was looking around the hangar. Fingers flexed, and arms and legs bent experimentally. The arms raised at the shoulder, and the giant robot twisted its torso from side to side.

"This is Armor Suit Harmony," Kenji's augmented voice boomed from speakers mounted in the robot's face. "Open the hangar doors."

The ceiling split overhead, and the roof opened up like a clamshell. The deep blue of the afternoon sky was visible beyond, with only a few puffy, white clouds scattered throughout. Alien ships streaked overhead, followed by fighters from the Japanese Air Self-Defense Force. When the roof finished opening, the giant robot, which stood nearly sixty feet tall, stepped away from the scaffolding that held it in place during maintenance and storage between missions. Enormous wings unfolded from Armor Suit Harmony's back.

"Stand clear," Kenji's voice issued once more from the robot's speakers. "Initiating launch procedure."

Rockets ignited in the battlesuit's feet. Smoke billowed for a moment, then the giant robot lifted into the air and flew into the afternoon sky over Tokyo.

The Black Cobra stared, wide-eyed, at the giant flying saucer that hovered over Manhattan. As he released a breath that he hadn't even realized he'd been holding, another costumed hero placed a reassuring hand on his shoulder.

Devon Collis was not the first Black Cobra; he was the fifth to bear the name, the latest in a long line of heroes. His grandfather, Bob Hornsby, had served first as the Cobra Kid, then as the third Black Cobra. Devon's mother, Renae Hornsby-Collis, succeeded her father in the mid-seventies, and had trained Devon for more than a decade, starting in the early nineties. He'd been the Cobra Kid to her Black Cobra until she retired and passed on the mantle to him, almost six years ago.

This was so far beyond anything he'd faced before, and he was overwhelmed. The man standing beside him squeezed his shoulder gently, then brought his hand back to his side.

"I understand your nervousness," the man said, "but we will get through this together. We are the Minutemen. We have a proud tradition of defending this city. Our home."

The Black Cobra turned his head to face the older man, and smiled weakly. The man had long, black hair and the darker skin tone that reflected his Native American heritage, and his red-and-gold costume also paid homage to his Comanche ancestors in its design, though it was far more skintight than anything they would have worn. Jacob Youngblood, better known as Speeding Arrow, was a speedster, and he carried a compound bow and a large quiver of arrows slung on his back, which he used for long-range combat.

Speeding Arrow was the most recent leader of the Minutemen, a team that traced its history back to the first superheroes in the mid-1950s. They had managed to remain when so many other heroes and teams were drafted and absorbed into the U.S. military in the early 1960s, due to the team's status as a state-level paramilitary organization, something which went back to the team's founding.

Speeding Arrow and Black Cobra watched the alien mothership in silence for a moment, before the older man brought them back to reality.

"Team Liberty will be joining us shortly," Speeding Arrow said of the U.S. military's elite, joint-forces, superhuman special operations unit, which was headquartered at Fort Wadsworth, in New York City. "This is going to be a fight for our very survival as a species. The people of this city are depending on us to protect them. Let's not disappoint them."

Chapter Sixteen

The fighting carried the Protectorate into a large room filled with dozens of Saurians at computer terminals that lined the walls. Other corridors were visible, branching away from openings in the walls around the perimeter of the room. Saurians scrambled for weapons and cover as the Protectorate pushed the defending force into the room ahead of them.

The center of the room was dominated by an enormous, sunken pit; at its center was a large, circular table that featured a holographic projection of the Earth, suspended in the air and rotating above it. Markings in an alien script that was indecipherable to the members of the Protectorate hovered around the globe, with lines from the alien words pointing toward the locations of cities around the planet.

"This looks like some kind of control room!" Pyre exclaimed as he unleashed another torrent of flame at the Saurians.

"It looks like they're coordinating the whole invasion from here," Nucleus agreed, nodding toward the hologram at the center of the room. One of the Saurians at the table was screeching in his native language, clearly giving orders, though they had no idea what it was that he was saying.

"Destroy everything!" Pyre yelled. "Maybe if we take this place out, we can stop them!"

—§—

Walter jogged toward Pershing Square. His car had gotten him as far as Dodger Stadium, which was honestly farther than he'd expected, but that was still two miles away from where he needed to be. The freeway was completely jammed, and he hadn't even tried to navigate that mess, but the surface streets were just as bad this close to downtown and…

He looked up as he jogged. The alien mothership was directly overhead and completely blotting out the sun. It was almost as dark as night underneath it, though enough light crept in from the sides that it wasn't quite that dark. People around him screamed and ran in terror. Smaller spacecraft darted between buildings and fired some kind of laser beams into the crowds. Explosions erupted wherever those beams struck, sending cars, people, and debris flying.

One of the ships was making an attack run on the street ahead of him. It was descending to take a point-blank shot, and heading straight toward him. He stopped, and looked around.

Walter was standing near the corner of First and Grand, between the Chandler Pavilion and the courthouse. The flying saucer was coming his way, and quickly, and if he didn't do something, he was as good as dead. There were trees lining the street. Large ones, on either side.

He thrust his hands out to either side, and reached out with his mind. In seconds, the trees began to move. Their trunks swelled and they shot into the air, arching across Grand Avenue. They met in the middle, and their branches began to weave together.

The Saurian pilot realized too late what was happening. He tried to pull up, but at the speed he was traveling, there simply wasn't time or space to maneuver. The small saucer slammed into the interwoven branches.

It lost control and slammed into the pavement below, then began to tumble down the street. It collided with abandoned cars, and careened into the LA County Tax Collector's office building. The wall shattered in the impact, and a cloud of dust and debris billowed into the air.

With a rush of displaced air, someone just… *appeared* next to him: a kid, probably in his late teens, with a bandana and goggles covering his head and face.

"Dude!" the kid exclaimed, eyes wide under his goggles. "That was freaking awesome!" Walter recoiled, shocked at the kid's sudden appearance. "Sorry," the kid said. "Super speed. It's like that sometimes." He extended a hand. "I'm Speedfreak."

Walter looked down for a moment, then took the kid's hand and began to shake it.

"Call me," he began, pausing for a moment before continuing with a grin, "Leafmaster."

Before either of them could say another word, screams drew their attention back to the tax collector's building. The kid seemed almost to vibrate for a second, then he looked at Walter.

"Three aliens," Speedfreak began, grabbing Walter by the arm. "They just got out of their ship. They look kind of disoriented. If we hurry, we can catch them before they hurt anybody else."

That was when Walter realized that everything around him had just... stopped. There weren't any screams. No sirens. Not even the sound of wind blowing. Speedfreak tugged at his arm.

"C'mon," the kid urged. "We're at superspeed, Leafmaster. We'll get there faster this way." Walter just nodded, and followed. Speedfreak led them toward the crash site at a brisk walk, then stopped when they were a few yards away from the aliens, who were armed with some kind of rifles.

"What's the plan?" Speedfreak asked.

Walter—*Leafmaster*—looked around. Then he looked at his belt, laden with pouches. Pouches full of seeds. He grinned, and pulled a handful out of one of the pouches. He threw them at the Saurians, but as soon as they left his hand, they just stopped and hovered in midair.

"Oh, sorry," Speedfreak said. "Only works when I'm touching you. I'll let you go and you'll go back to normal speed." An instant later, the seeds shot through the air, and landed at the Saurians' feet.

Leafmaster thrust his hands out toward the Saurians, and where the seeds had fallen on the ground, vines erupted. They ensnared the reptilian creatures, an enormous maw appearing from each group of vines. The vines curled tight, and delivered the Saurians into the waiting, toothy mouths.

"Is," Speedfreak began, then corrected himself. "Are those...?"

"Giant Venus flytraps," Leafmaster grinned. "Feed me, Seymour."

Missiles shot out from the launchers mounted in the shoulders of Armor Suit Harmony. They streaked through the sky, pinwheeling as they locked on to their targets and took chase. Moments later, they exploded upon impact with one of the dozens of small Saurian ships in the skies above Tokyo.

Fighter jets from the Air Self-Defense Force streaked past from multiple directions, each chasing a target of its own. Other super-powered heroes flew past as well, all smaller and more maneuverable than the giant battlesuit, but not as heavily armed.

Kenji Tanaka may not have been able to fly under his own power, or to project beams of energy from his body like some of the heroes around him, but he possessed one of the greatest minds on the planet. He had designed the Armor Suit technology, inspired by the anime that he had grown up watching, inventing a number of supplemental technologies in the process that had made him wealthy enough to build and maintain the battlesuit in the first place.

Kenji watched as the flying saucer he had targeted disappeared from his sensor display, then chose another target. With dozens of the ships in the air, attacking the city below, that didn't take him very long.

The rockets in the feet of the battlesuit ignited, and Armor Suit Harmony sped across the sky toward Kenji's target. The arms reached around as he flew, and extracted another of the suit's formidable weapons from its storage compartment. Servos whirred and panels moved, locking into place in a new configuration. The arms came back together in front of the suit as it came to rest relative to the saucer, holding a gargantuan sword, easily thirty feet long, in a ready stance.

Kenji flipped switches and grabbed his controls. The suit surged forward, bringing the sword down against the saucer with a resounding boom of metal against metal.

— § —

Graviton spun around, her right arm extended, and a Saurian launched through the air. The reptilian creature soared from a position near the doorway on the opposite side of the room from Graviton, passed through the holographic projection of Earth, and crashed, headfirst, into one of the freestanding computer terminals mounted around the perimeter of the pit, on the opposite side of the room from where he had been a moment earlier. The metal casing on the device crumpled instantly, and sparks flew from the electronics within as the Saurian's body went limp, his head buried deep within.

Another Saurian soldier stared in shock at the scene that had just unfolded beside him. Looking up from the limp body at his feet, he raised a rifle to his shoulder and brought it to bear. He took aim at Graviton, and fired.

The blast stopped, inches away from the end of his weapon's barrel. Sphere stared at him, his hand extended, clawlike, in furious concentration. The control panel beside the Saurian began to crumple, and ripped away from the floor where it had been mounted. The control panel slammed into the side of the Saurian, who was suddenly struck from the opposite side by an invisible barrier.

The barrier continued to contract, its diameter shrinking at an accelerated rate. In an instant, the two Saurians, and the control panel, were reduced to a ball less than a foot in diameter. Sphere released the forcefield, and it dropped, slowly in the lunar gravity, to the floor with a dull thud.

Nucleus and Plasmid stood back to back, waves of Saurians approaching from corridors on either side of the room. They unleashed their plasma at the Saurians, who simply kept coming from the doorways. Nearby, Versipellis, who had long since shifted almost entirely into his armored form, easily slashed through the attacking Saurians with his razor-like claws. Psyche pulled one of the fallen Saurians' rifles to her with her telekinesis, took a moment to familiarize herself with the weapon, which had a trigger mechanism oddly similar to a human rifle, and began to open fire on the control consoles around her.

Pyre leaped into the air and advanced on the table at the center of the room. He dodged and weaved as the lone Saurian who remained at the table fired at him with a pistol of some kind. Pyre unleashed a torrent of flame, which engulfed the Saurian leader. He fell to the ground, but his inhuman shrieks stopped before Pyre landed atop the table a moment later.

"Clear the room!" Pyre yelled over the din of combat. His entire body began to glow, and tongues of flame licked out from his arms, legs, chest, and head. The flames spread, and within seconds, his entire body was a pillar of fire. The heat grew steadily more intense, and he lifted into the air above the table once again as the plastics on its surface began to melt.

The rest of the team ducked into open corridors nearby, and soon the Saurian soldiers followed suit. Moments later, as they rushed to find corners to take cover behind, the flames surrounding Pyre exploded outward. Plastics and glass melted. Metal grew soft and sagged. The air was utterly consumed in the flame.

Just as quickly as it began, the flames vanished. There was a rush of wind as air was sucked into the room to fill the sudden vacuum. A new alarm joined the cacophony of noises that had filled the base since the attack had begun.

— § —

Without warning, the smaller Saurian ships began flying erratically. Those near the ground crashed, impacting the pavement and buildings at velocities far too fast to have been planned. Something had happened, but Sentinel had no idea what that was. The National Guard was on site, and several fighters from the Air National Guard had joined Sentinel in engaging the alien ships. The tide had turned, and he wasn't going to look a gift horse in the mouth.

Below, he could see Speedfreak and another person he didn't recognize. They were both obviously fighting against the aliens, attacking a group of Saurians as they exited their downed ship. But there were still civilians on the street, and helping the other would-be hero was distracting Speedfreak from the evacuation.

Sentinel landed near the pair, at the edge of Pershing Square, near the corner of Fifth and Olive. Before he could say anything to them, however, he saw another saucer lose control and begin a ballistic descent toward the ground. Smoke billowed from the underside of the craft, and a fighter jet streaked past, its engine roaring.

"Clear the street, kid!" Sentinel called as he launched himself back into the air. "I'll slow this thing down!"

Sentinel slammed into the flying saucer, his fingers digging into the edge of the ship. He pushed against it, straining, but it was falling fast, and it was big.

His feet slammed into the ground. Bricks shattered and flew as he and the wayward saucer drove a furrow into Pershing Square. They slid for nearly a dozen yards, but they were slowing.

Finally, they stopped. Slowly, gently, Sentinel lowered the damaged craft to the shattered ground. He breathed a heavy sigh of relief.

— § —

The Iron Lady dodged and weaved as one of the flying saucers chased her through the London streets. The property damage they had wrought had been terrible, but it could have been far worse.

She and the other heroes were drawing their attention, allowing time for the civilian population to escape. Civilian casualties had been kept to a minimum, far fewer than they would have been otherwise. Jets had streaked in from the Royal Air Force, backing the heroes up and taking on the alien craft, but it was hard for them to maneuver between buildings, and the aliens knew it.

Most of the flying saucers were sticking close to their mothership, dodging and weaving between buildings under its protective shadow. Left with no other targets, the RAF had focused on the mothership itself, and explosions could be heard from the top of that massive ship, echoing in the streets below.

The heroes had landed a few lucky shots, and a handful of the flying saucers had been damaged, but the coordination of their movements had proved to be a significant challenge. The fighting had been intense, but had proved to be nearly a stalemate, with the Saurians taking only light losses. If they could just lure the smaller ships out into the open, the RAF could pick them off easily.

She rounded a corner, hoping that she could get this particular alien pilot to focus on her to the exclusion of his surroundings. She was leading him on a merry chase, slowly coaxing him closer and closer to the edge of the mothership's shadow.

As she rounded the corner, she saw Pixie Pristine zip past her in the opposite direction. She and Pixie had been trying to use the same tactic, and had apparently picked the same corner to round. The Iron Lady nearly collided with the saucer that had been chasing Pixie, and cut her suit's rockets for an instant, so that she dropped toward the ground like a stone.

Overhead, the two saucers collided in a massive fireball as the Iron Lady reignited her rockets. She hovered mere feet above the pavement, shielding herself from falling debris with the gauntlets on her forearms.

Something had interrupted their coordinated flight patterns, the Iron Lady realized. They could yet win this, after all.

Chapter Seventeen

Armor Suit Harmony landed atop the Saurian mothership, sword in hand. The smaller saucers were clearly trying to swarm toward the battlesuit in order to protect their mothership, but the fighter jets and the other heroes were running enough interference that Kenji was able to land the suit with little trouble.

Kenji slashed at the tough metal of the ship's exterior skin. His ammunition had been all but exhausted while fighting the smaller ships, but that wasn't an issue where his sword was concerned.

A furrow in the metal began to grow where his sword slashed across the top of the giant saucer-shaped craft. Eventually, that wore down to a weakened point that his suit's sensors identified. Kenji stopped slashing at the saucer, and adjusted his suit's grip on the sword, spinning the handle in its giant hands.

Bracing the suit with its legs spread apart, Kenji flipped a switch and enormous bolts drove down into the hull of the ship from the feet of the battlesuit, locking it into place. Kenji brought the sword up above the suit's head in a two-handed grip, its blade pointing downward.

The sword shot down with incredible speed and force, directly onto the weakened point in the hull that Kenji had created moments earlier. The point drove through the hull with a deafening screech of tearing metal. The suit's hydraulics and servos continued to push the sword down into the alien craft, leaving destruction in its wake.

Kenji felt the ship lurch, his stomach becoming queasy in a moment of freefall. He frantically adjusted his controls, and the battlesuit began to pull the thirty-foot sword from the Saurian vessel. The angle was slightly different on exit, and it caused more damage on the way out.

Once the sword was free, Kenji detonated the explosive bolts that had secured Armor Suit Harmony to the Saurian vessel. He ignited the rockets in the suit's feet, and shot into the air as the giant flying saucer listed to one side and began a slow descent toward the ground.

The sword folded back into its storage configuration, and Kenji locked it back into place. Turning his suit, he extended the arms, and rocketed back toward the falling spacecraft. The suit's hands crushed the hull of the ship where they came into contact, and Kenji began to push the ship away.

The spacecraft was going to hit the ground, but Kenji would ensure that it didn't do so while it was still hovering over the city.

— § —

The ground shook underneath the Protectorate's feet as they made their way back to the airlock where they had entered the Saurian base.

The corridors were in chaos. Saurians rushed in multiple directions, all but ignoring the humans. The damage had been done, and the invasion had failed. With a low rumble, the ground shook once more.

The Saurians were abandoning the base. Escaping spacecraft launched every few seconds, with enough force that the entire complex shook. None of the fleeing Saurians seemed interested in pressing the fight with the humans who remained in their midst. Their leaders were dead, the battle lost. All that remained for them was to retreat and regroup.

By the time the Protectorate reached the airlock, the corridors were virtually deserted in that part of the base. They found their spacesuits untouched, still concealed in the storage compartments where the team had left them. They quickly donned their suits, and checked one another to ensure there were no tears or unfastened seals before entering the airlock.

Once inside, the airlock cycled to vacuum with impressive speed. Plasmid opened the exterior hatch and the group exited onto the lunar surface. Just as when they first entered, there were heavy shadows surrounding the Saurian base.

This part of the moon was near the terminator—the edge of the area currently being illuminated by the sun—and was on the side opposite the Earth, to aid in concealing it from casual view by human observers. The sky above was black, with few stars visible thanks to the bright reflection of the sun's rays off of the lunar surface, and the sun itself was low to the horizon.

Their rover was concealed in one of the long shadows nearby, and the group of humans made their way back to it as quickly as they could. With no atmosphere, there were no particles to diffuse and refract the sunlight, and the shadows were utterly dark.

Their suits were equipped with lights to help cut through the darkness, but even those only lit small parts of the area ahead of them. They knew, roughly, where they had left the rover, but even then it took several tense minutes to find it in the obsidian depths of the shadow that they had used to conceal it.

Looking back toward the Saurian base, they saw saucer ships streaking away, into the jet black sky. They clambered back into the rover in twos and threes, its airlock unable to accommodate more due to its diminutive size, a process that took an agonizingly long time due to the need to cycle the air in and out of the small chamber.

Once everyone was inside and all of their gear had been securely stowed, they took a quick accounting. Their losses had been surprisingly light. Of the dozen that had entered the base, only two had fallen in the fighting, both from the Armstrong security detachment.

The ninety-minute drive back to where they had left the suborbital hopper passed in almost total silence as everyone processed what they had just been through.

— § —

Leafmaster sat on a grassy area in Pershing Square, and dropped his head in his hands as he rested his elbows on his knees. He tried not to think about how terrified he had been, and just focused on breathing. In. Out. As long as he just thought about breathing, he wouldn't have to think about what he had just survived.

In. Out.

In. Out.

"Are you all right, sir?"

Leafmaster jumped in surprise, half spinning where he sat. He looked around, frantically, and saw someone kneeling down in front of him.

"I'm sorry," the man—Sentinel—said gently. "I didn't mean to startle you." He paused, waiting while Leafmaster regained his composure and control of his breathing.

"Speedfreak said you called yourself Leafmaster," Sentinel continued finally, hooking a thumb over his shoulder to indicate the young speedster standing several feet behind him, a worried expression on his face that even his face-concealing goggles couldn't hide.

Leafmaster nodded, unable to force his mouth to produce sounds. Sentinel's expression changed slightly, and he gave a knowing nod.

"First big fight?" Sentinel asked. Leafmaster nodded again. "I thought so. First time is always the worst, once the adrenaline wears off."

Sentinel moved and sat down at Leafmaster's right side. He looked at the younger man, and continued, "It'll pass. You'll be okay, eventually, but it's going to be rough for a while. I'll stay here with you, until you're feeling ready to move, if that's all right."

Leafmaster blinked, wide-eyed, at Sentinel for a moment, then nodded.

"It's going to be all right," Sentinel said, and placed a reassuring hand on Leafmaster's shoulder.

—§—

The Iron Lady stared at the scene unfolding directly above her as she landed on the grounds near Big Ben. The smaller alien ships were flying back to the safety of the mothership, and were beginning to dock within the larger vessel once more.

The tide of the battle had suddenly turned, and now the aliens were fleeing back to their mothership just as quickly.

At first, they had worried that it was the first phase of a new attack, but word began to filter in from around the world that the sudden interruption in the Saurians' ability to coordinate their attacks was happening on a global scale.

Even as the last of the smaller ships maneuvered into position to dock within the larger vessel, the mothership began to climb into the sky. Within minutes, it had disappeared from view.

Several yards away, she saw the MI5 agents who called themselves the Bollocks. The woman with the wings, Bird, had been injured; during the chaos toward the end, an out-of-control saucer had clipped her right wing, and she'd plummeted nearly fifty feet to the pavement below. The other two, Gaffer and Bloke, were at her side as paramedics placed her on a gurney and loaded her into an ambulance. Regardless of her first impression of them, they'd fought hard to defend London and, for that at least, had earned the Iron Lady's respect.

Further in the distance, she noticed Pixie Pristine standing atop one of the downed saucers. The Iron Lady activated her suit's thrusters, closing the distance in a matter of seconds. She dropped to the ground a few feet from the edge of the debris, the joined her sidekick on foot.

"Something the matter?" the Iron Lady asked as she stepped up beside the younger woman.

Pixie Pristine waved a hand at the shattered remains of the saucer. "Lord Albion smashed through this one," Pixie replied. "Notice anything?"

The Iron Lady looked at the debris. She saw torn and twisted metal from the craft's hull and support skeleton, wiring, and the remains of electronics that were used to control the craft. All of which she would have expected.

And then she realized what her sidekick was showing her. She saw what *wasn't* there.

— § —

The Black Cobra sat on the edge of the rooftop, his back against the wall, his boots crunching the gravel surface as he shifted his feet in front of himself. He looked up in exhausted silence and watched the Saurian mothership recede into the sky.

He heard the gravel crunching under someone's boots as they walked toward him, but didn't bother to look at who it was. He was just too exhausted to move. Whoever it was stopped next to him, then dropped down to sit on the rooftop next to him.

"Good work out there, kid," a man's voice said. The voice was familiar, but he couldn't place it. "Your grandpa would've been proud."

The Black Cobra finally turned his head. How could anyone know what his grandfather would have thought? Instantly, he realized who had joined him on the rooftop.

"Strongman!" the Black Cobra blurted in surprise. The older man grinned and offered his hand to the young hero.

"Pleasure to finally meet you, kid," Strongman said as the Black Cobra shook his hand. Even at eighty-two years of age, the elder hero had a powerful grip. "But it's just Percy now. I retired before you were even born."

The Black Cobra nodded, dumbstruck to be meeting Percy van Norton, one of the world's first superheroes. He let go of the older man's hand, still staring. Van Norton chuckled.

"Y'know," van Norton said, looking around, "I met the first Black Cobra on a rooftop a lot like this one, back in 1954." He looked back at the current holder of the Black Cobra mantle. "He would've been your... what, grand-uncle? Great uncle? Your grandpa's brother, anyway, whatever that's called."

"Yes, sir," the Black Cobra said. "You were all in the Minutemen together. The *first* Minutemen."

Van Norton nodded. "They were good men," he said. "You and your mom have done them proud."

"That means a lot, sir," the Black Cobra said. "Thank you." His eyes narrowed. "What are you doing out here, sir?"

"New York's my home, too," van Norton replied, raising an eyebrow with a grin. "No way I'm gonna let a bunch of lizards wreck it."

— § —

A staff officer handed a piece of paper to General Welsh, which he read quickly before clearing his throat to get the attention of the other members of the Joint Chiefs of Staff.

"I've just received word from Space Command," Welsh began, once he had their attention. "Satellite telemetry confirms the Saurian ships have left the atmosphere and are on course for a return trip to Mars. The ships leaving their moon base are on course to rendezvous with the rest of their fleet."

Cheers erupted throughout the situation room. After a moment, General Dunford raised a hand, and the room was quiet once more.

"How many are still on the ground?" Dunford asked.

"We have confirmation," Welsh began, "of two motherships brought down: Tokyo and Sydney. There's an unconfirmed report that one went down in Beijing, as well."

"And their ground forces?" Dunford asked.

"Minimal ground forces deployed," replied General Mark Milley, the Chief of Staff of the Army. Much like the other generals, he was in his fifties, and kept his graying hair trimmed short in a high-and-tight cut. "Nearly all of those were recalled to the motherships before they left. The only ones left behind were dead or disabled and unable to retreat."

"I have reports of prisoners," added General Grass, the head of the National Guard Bureau.

Dunford nodded. He was certain of one thing: eventually, the enemy would return, and they needed to be better prepared for that day.

Chapter Eighteen

As the Protectorate stepped into the Central Gardens after returning to Armstrong Colony, applause filled the air. The balconies overlooking the verdant space were lined with colonists, who had come to cheer for the returning heroes. Somewhat sheepishly, Pyre began waving as he looked around, taking in the sight.

A young woman with raven-black hair and mahogany skin came bounding across the open space of the gardens, her leaps in the fractional lunar gravity carrying her even faster than if she had been running on Earth. She collided with Plasmid, who caught her, barely avoiding being knocked over himself in the process. The others spun in surprise. Was someone attacking?

Plasmid wrapped his arms around the woman and they kissed. When she pulled back, she was laughing, and they were both smiling. Plasmid turned his head toward Nucleus, who was standing at his side, eyebrows raised and eyes wide in surprise.

"David," Plasmid began, "this is Michaela."

"The woman you told me about," Nucleus nodded, comprehension dawning.

"Michaela," Plasmid continued, turning his head to face her, "this is my brother, David."

Nucleus extended a hand. When Michaela began to shake his hand, he said, "Pleasure to meet you."

"You, too," Michaela said. She withdrew her hand, then looked at Plasmid once again. "Don, I'm sorry I couldn't meet you at the gate, but things got pretty crazy while you were gone."

"That's okay," Plasmid said, his growing concern evident in his voice. He knew that Michaela worked in the colony's hospital. "Is everything all right?"

"Yes!" she replied enthusiastically. "Administrator Jefferson wanted me to be the one to tell you, and he wants me to bring all of you to see him in his office before everyone goes back to Earth."

"Tell me what?" Plasmid asked.

"It's the president," Michaela said. Plasmid's brow furrowed for a moment, not following where her explanation was going. "He's giving you a pardon," she continued a moment later, "in recognition for helping to beat the aliens!"

Plasmid blinked several times, his eyes wide. Nucleus clapped him on the back, grinning.

"That's great!" Nucleus said. "You can go back home!"

Plasmid looked at Nucleus, his brow still furrowed. He looked back at Michaela, then pulled her close, and looked back at his brother, joining in everyone's smiles.

"I *am* home," Plasmid said.

— § —

The next day, Pyre stepped off of the helipad atop the Chambers Casino and Resort. His father was waiting for him at the base of the stairs, near the roof access doorway. As soon as Pyre was close enough, Max grabbed hold of him and embraced his son.

"Thank God you're all right, John," Max said, wrapping his arms around the young hero.

Pyre pulled away just far enough so that he could look his father in the eye. "You too, dad," he said. "Have you heard from mom?"

"And then some," Max grimaced. He took a breath and continued, "She's fine."

"She worries," Pyre said.

Max nodded and embraced his son again. After a moment, he pulled away. "I have to get back to the office," he said. "We'll need to talk to the press soon. Get yourselves ready."

"I understand," Pyre nodded. "We'll be ready."

Max turned and made his way back into the building. He descended several floors, the elevator taking him directly from the Protectorate's headquarters facilities to his office within the resort. He strode past his secretary, Marcia, and entered his office proper, where he found a woman with bright red hair and an immaculate gray business suit waiting for him, seated in the chair across from his desk.

"I should have expected to find you here, Tempora," Max said, shutting the door behind him and moving briskly to take his seat behind his desk.

"This threat has passed," Tempora said.

"*This* threat," Max echoed.

Tempora sighed almost imperceptibly. "There are many more things to come."

"And you'll be there," Max shot back in exasperation, "to spoon-feed me just enough to be useful."

"I'm sorry," Tempora said, and she honestly looked contrite, "but I can't tell you everything. I swear to you, though, I would never do anything to harm you or your family."

Max leaned back, crossing his arms. He studied her through narrowed eyes. "Who are you?" he demanded.

Tempora's gaze fell to the floor. "You'll find out," she said, sadly. "Soon."

—§—

"Oh," a man's voice said, muffled and slightly echoing from deep within the wreckage of the Saurian mothership that had crashed in Sydney, Australia. "Oh, *that's* interesting."

In the chaos of the battle, shortly after the Saurians' communications network was disrupted by the Protectorate, several of the smaller saucers crashed into the larger ship. The rips in its hull's armor plating left it vulnerable to attack, and a concentrated volley of artillery fire from both the Australian Royal Navy's defensive picket and the nearby U.S. Navy's Carrier Strike Group 9, led by the *Nimitz*-class aircraft carrier U.S.S. *Theodore Roosevelt*. The concentrated attack crippled the alien mothership, and sent it crashing into Sydney Harbor, where it narrowly avoided a collision with the famous Sydney Opera House.

Shipping lanes in and out of the harbor were severely disrupted, but teams of scientists were swarming over the wreckage, which, despite having been partially submerged, was largely intact, and was already proving to be a treasure trove of secrets.

"What have you found?" a woman's voice called out. A moment later, her head poked out from an open doorway, looking into the empty corridor. "Shawn?" she asked. There was no reply.

The ship had settled into the harbor at a twenty-degree angle, so it required an effort for the woman to exit the room that she was in, and to enter the darkened corridor. She was thin and had long, dark brown hair and alabaster skin. She was dressed in tan cargo pants, a button-up work shirt, and heavy, brown work boots, and she braced herself against the steeply-angled wall with one hand as she carefully made her way to the next open door, a chemical light stick in her other hand glowing a soft, cool green.

"Shawn!" she called, leaning over the open doorway of the next room. When no one answered, she tried again. "Dr. McCrackin! What did you find?"

Legs clad in olive drab cargo pants and tan work boots of a similar style flopped in a surprised spasm under a console at the far end of the room, and a moment later, a voice squeaked, "Who—who's there?!"

The woman rolled her eyes. "It's Denise."

"Oh!" the voice—belonging to Dr. Shawn McCrackin—replied, and he began to worm his way out from under the console to face his colleague. "Dr. Urbane! This is incredible! I think it explains why the smaller ships started crashing!"

"What does?" Urbane asked, then sighed. "I have no idea what you're on about. Walk me through it."

"They were drones!" McCrackin exclaimed as he finished pulling himself out from under the console and sat up, bracing his back against the far wall. He mussed his curly, bright red—almost orange—hair and pushed his thick glasses higher up on the bridge of his nose. "Most of them, anyway. This console was a control unit for them, but it looks like some kind of power surge overloaded it. Probably feedback from when the Protectorate blew up the control hub on the moon."

"Oh," Urbane said, her shoulders slumping slightly in disappointment. "We already *have* drone technology."

"Not like this," McCrackin said. "And now we know about this control network for next time. We could jam their signals or hack into it or something."

Urbane turned and began to work her way back to the other room that she had come from. "That's great, Shawn," she said, rolling her eyes again once her back was turned. "Let's keep looking for something that we *don't* already have yet."

—§—

"Enough about my taxes," the man on the stage said, gripping the podium. "I'm a businessman. I run businesses. I *know* business. I know that if I ran my business the way this administration has been running things, I'd be *out* of business. My opponent just wants to keep doing business the way this administration's been doing business. And that's not good business. I *know* good business."

"Mr. Davidson," the moderator began, mildly exasperated, but the candidate in this latest presidential debate, Alexander Davidson, cut him off.

"Look," Davidson said, "we were attacked. By *aliens*. This administration knew it. They knew the Martians were there the whole time, and they never told us! We could've been ready!"

"We fought them off," the moderator began, but Davidson cut him off again before he could redirect the debate back to the original question.

"We almost didn't," Davidson said, and looked accusingly at his counterpart on the stage, former Secretary of State Hillary Clinton. "This administration was more worried about keeping its secrets and buying votes with handouts. We need to focus on our security. Our borders. Our troops. No more secrets. No more helping countries that don't help us. We need to look out for America first."

"Secretary Clinton," the moderator began, resigned to not addressing the original question, "would you like to—"

"I'm not done yet," Davidson interrupted once again.

"Yes, you are, sir," the moderator snapped, his composure faltering. "Madame Secretary..."

— § —

The building exploded. A cloud of debris several stories tall rocketed outward, coating everything in fine sand and choking the air with dust. As the patter of debris striking the ground began to still, screams and cries broke the momentary silence.

Incredibly, a man stood at the center of the pile of rubble that was once a building on the outskirts of Baghdad. He seemed utterly undisturbed by the chaos that surrounded him, and none of the debris marred his light-colored robes, his matching turban, or his long, dark beard. His narrowed eyes blazed with righteous anger for a moment, before he closed them and took a long, deep breath.

Releasing the breath and reopening his eyes, he stilled his face into a serene mask, then stepped carefully through the remains of the building, never once losing his footing on the loose piles of debris and soft chunks of pulverized human remains. Once clear of the rubble, he stopped as a trio of Iraqi soldiers rushed into the dust-choked area.

"Halt!" one of the soldiers ordered in Arabic as the trio brought their weapons to bear on the man. His unhurried, almost serene pace in the immediate aftermath of such a devastating explosion was incredibly suspicious, and they were taking no chances. They had seen far too much in their lifetimes to be anything less than wary in such a scenario.

The soldiers' rifles flew from their hands, clattering to the ground a dozen yards away. The soldiers recoiled in horror, backing away slowly. There had been reports of superhumans operating with several of the terrorist groups that still plagued the country in the wake of the American invasion more than a decade earlier. They were just assigned as a police patrol, and weren't equipped to take on a threat like that.

"You will deliver a message for me," the man said to them in Arabic. He hadn't so much as raised a finger, and his chin was held high as he spoke. "Tell your superiors that their rule is coming to an end. Their supplication to the Western infidels is an abomination. I and my followers are here to cleanse the world of the impure."

The soldiers retreated to one side while the man strode forward. As he passed them, he added, "I am the *yad Allahi*." The Hand of God. He disappeared from view a moment later, concealed in the thick cloud of dust.

Team Liberty vs. the Martians

CHAPTER ONE

June 1975

Percy van Norton looked up from the overstuffed chair in his study as someone walked into the room through the door behind him. He turned in his seat, and immediately noticed the man was wearing an Army Class A uniform, which strongly resembled a dark green business suit adorned with nearly two dozen ribbons above his left breast pocket and the double silver bars of a captain's insignia on his shoulders. A black nametag with white letters was pinned to the jacket above his right breast pocket.

"Captain Holton," van Norton said, rising to his feet and extending his right hand in greeting. "Good to see you, sir. What brings you here?"

Tod Holton, a fairly young man in his late twenties with black hair and piercing blue eyes, was the third man to use the code name Captain Freedom. Van Norton, as Strongman, had served with the original Captain Freedom, Don Wright, at the end of the Korean War. Wright left the military several years later, however, and took over the publication of the *New York Daily Bulletin*, a newspaper that had been in his family for generations. He was succeeded in the role by John Grayson, who led the team until 1967, when Holton took over as the team's operational commander.

Holton took van Norton's hand and gave it a vigorous shake. "Straight to the point," he said. "I always liked that about you, sergeant."

"I'm a civilian again, sir," van Norton said gently. "Been out since the war ended."

"Old habits," Holton said. "We've got a situation and could use your expertise."

"Am I being recalled to active duty?" van Norton asked.

"No," Holton said. "You'll be brought on as a civilian advisor. Your clearances are still up to date. Just report to the Bunker tomorrow morning, oh-eight-hundred hours. Everyone will be briefed at that time."

Van Norton nodded. "I'll be there."

The two shook hands once again, and Holton made his exit.

Sighing, van Norton fell back into his chair. Just when he thought he was out, the government came and pulled him back in. The Vietnam War had ended, at least for him, more than two years ago, when the United States signed the Paris Accords and recalled all of its military forces from the country. Without U.S. aid, the South Vietnamese forces had been overrun, and Saigon had fallen just days earlier.

He'd come back to a less-than-appreciative homecoming. People screamed insults at him and spit on him when he was in uniform. It was a far cry from the reception he had when he appeared in costume as Strongman. It pained him to admit that there was a part of him that was glad he didn't have to wear the uniform again for the mission that Captain Holton had just recruited him to participate in.

During the war, van Norton had served under Holton's command as part of Team Liberty, the United States military's elite, joint-forces superhuman strike force. He had been part of the team at its inception during the final months of the Korean War, but left the military soon after that conflict ended. When the Vietnam War escalated nearly a decade ago, van Norton was recalled to active duty under the provisions of the Superhuman Induction Act, which had been passed in the wake of the Cuban Missile Crisis.

Despite this, Team Liberty once again never deployed in combat in Vietnam. Congress brought them all together, sent them to the war zone... and had them sit on their hands for four years. The team was kept in reserve, in the unlikely event that the Soviets would deploy their own superhumans first, and never allowed to participate because of the fear of nuclear retaliation by the Soviet Union, should the United States be the first to deploy its superhumans.

Realizing that he had an early morning ahead of him, van Norton stood and left the room. He made his way through the hallways of his family's estate, his footsteps echoing off the walls, tracing his path to his bedroom.

— § —

Van Norton stepped out of the elevator that had been concealed within an administration building's supply closet, and was greeted by the familiar sight of a long, narrow tunnel with a pair of M2 "Ma Deuce" .50 caliber machine guns pointed at him from the other end. He presented his identification to the guard behind the armored fighting position between the gun emplacements, and the door to his right buzzed as the locking mechanism disengaged.

Inside, he found another room with another guard checkpoint, and three more elevators. A guard within inspected the contents of the bag van Norton carried, then, satisfied that there was nothing dangerous within, waved him on to continue. Using the middle elevator, he descended further, and exited into what looked like a typical office building's hallway. To his right, doors opened into offices and conference rooms. To his left, what appeared to be large windows were actually little more than picture frames, with backlit photographs simulating a view from an office tower.

Van Norton turned into the conference room four doors down from the elevator. Inside, a dozen people were already seated around the large table that dominated the center of the room. They all wore olive drab military uniforms and chatted quietly with one another, while one of them sorted paperwork at the podium mounted at the far end of the table.

"Strongman!" a voice called from the table, and a hand shot up in a wave, then beckoned him forward. "Get the hell over here!" Next to the man—whom van Norton now recognized as one of his former teammates, Chuck Hardy, who went by the code name Samson—was an unoccupied seat, which he patted by way of invitation with a toothy grin that contrasted strongly against his dark-skinned face.

Dropping his bag along the wall behind the chair, van Norton approached his former comrade in arms. "Hardy!" he exclaimed. "You son of a bitch." What began as a handshake quickly became an impromptu arm wrestling bout. Hardy's forearm began to shake as each struggled to push the other's hand into submission. "What's the matter?" van Norton asked, glancing playfully at their grasped hands. "Command Chief duties got you pushing too many pencils?"

"Command *Master* Chief," Hardy corrected with a grin. "You damned well know Navy ratings, you Army puke." He glanced at their hands. "Give up yet?"

"Atten-*hut!*" a voice called out before van Norton could deliver a retort to his old friend. Everyone at the table shot out of their chairs and stood at attention, their posture rigid, their eyes locked forward. Even though he was no longer required to observe the military custom as a civilian, van Norton found himself coming to the position of attention out of reflex borne from years of training and habit.

"As you were," Captain Holton said as he crossed the room for the podium at the head of the table. As everyone took their seats, Holton looked at the faces of the men before him. After a moment to allow everyone to settle into place, Holt began the briefing.

"Late yesterday afternoon," Holton began, "an unidentified craft was intercepted in Alaskan airspace, after it crossed over from Soviet territory. Fighters from Elmendorf Air Force Base intercepted the craft, which did not match anything known to be in the Soviet arsenal. The fighters pursued the craft through a thunderstorm, where it was struck by lightning and crashed just outside U.S. territory, in international waters in the Bering Sea. It's currently resting on the edge of the continental shelf, north of the Aleutian Islands."

An image appeared on the projector screen behind Holton. It was an old, grainy, black-and-white photo of a saucer-shaped craft. It was made of a reflective metal and seemed to be in a warehouse of some kind. "We captured," Holton continued, indicating the craft on the screen behind him with his left hand, "a smaller type of these vehicles in 1947, when one crashed outside of Roswell, New Mexico, under similar circumstances."

Everyone at the table exchanged looks of surprise and disbelief. Only military discipline kept them all from putting their thoughts to words. "Sir," van Norton interrupted after a moment, "is that... a flying saucer?"

"It is," Holton confirmed. "And yes, there are aliens."

"Don't tell me," van Norton said. "Little green men from Mars."

Holton shifted his weight, and pursed his lips uncomfortably. "Well, they're not little." He nodded to the adjutant at the slide projector, and a moment later, the image changed to another black-and-white photo, this time of a reptilian looking creature lying on a surgical table. "We call them Saurians," Holton explained. "They seem to be a couple hundred years ahead of us, technologically, and they really do come from Mars. We don't know how, but testing performed on the remains of the Saurians recovered in 1947 indicate that, somehow, they seem to be related to dinosaurs."

This time, even the ingrained military discipline failed the assembled team, and muttered curses and exclamations of disbelief filled the room. Holton allowed the interruption for a few moments, then brought the briefing back to order.

"These ships of theirs," he began, and the voices quickly quieted, "represent a significant asset. We cannot allow the Russians to get their hands on this ship. We know they are already scrambling their own mission to intercept and retrieve the ship and its technology. We have a Coast Guard cutter on station at the crash site, but it's only a matter of time before the Russians send ships of their own to drive it off. It's our job to get in, secure the site, and bring that ship back into American territory."

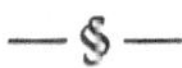

After the briefing ended, van Norton joined the other members of the team as they readied themselves for the mission. While the others packed uniforms appropriate for the underwater, arctic conditions, van Norton donned his signature costume as Strongman, founding member of the superhero team the Minutemen. His invulnerable skin meant that the pressure and freezing ocean temperatures of the Bering Strait would have little effect on him, and his costume was nearly as skin tight, so an insulated wet suit was superfluous in his case.

Strongman's brightly-colored costume stood out starkly from the sea of green military uniforms. It was a predominantly dark blue sleeveless jacket and trunks, with bright yellow tights and cape, and an inverted yellow triangle across his chest. His arms were bare, and blue boots matched his jacket and trunks.

"Looking sharp," Hardy said, his voice thick with sarcasm as he looked Strongman over.

"It's what all the kids are wearing these days," Strongman retorted.

Once they had all changed into their mission gear, the team proceeded to the armory, several levels down within the Bunker. The facility had originally been built underneath Fort Wadsworth, an Army facility on the outskirts of New York City, as a secret fallout shelter for government VIPs in the early 1950s, after the Soviet Union detonated its first nuclear devices. When Team Liberty was founded in the final months of the Korean War, the shelter was repurposed as their headquarters facility, and expanded upon over the next two decades.

It now boasted extensive specialized vehicle and weapons storage facilities, training areas for the team to practice their superpowered combat skills in total secrecy, and support facilities that allowed them to remain within the Bunker for weeks at a time without resupply. All of the team and their support personnel had living quarters within the Bunker, but married personnel lived in base housing above ground, since their families weren't cleared to even know of the Bunker's existence.

At the armory, each member of the team was issued their weapons for the mission, tailored for their role within the team and their individual superpowers. Strongman was issued a Colt M1911A1 .45 caliber semiautomatic pistol, with an ample supply of ammunition, as well as a number of grenades. Once everyone had their gear, it was packed onto a pallet and moved to the vehicle hangar for loading onto the trucks that would take them to their waiting flight at JFK airport.

After their gear was situated, it was just past noon, and the team headed for a quick meal at the Bunker's dining facility. One of the perks of the team was that the food was excellent by military standards. Strongman carried his tray from the serving line and quickly spotted his old friend, Hardy, sitting at a nearby table with several other members of the team. A seat sat empty next to him, clearly reserved for him by Hardy.

Strongman joined the others at the table. Most of them he knew from his time with the team during the war, but there were a few that he didn't recognize. They ate quickly, keeping conversation to a minimum, as they knew they were on a tight schedule to depart. When they had finished their meals, they returned their trays to the collection window in the wall by the kitchen.

With everyone and their gear loaded, a pair of trucks drove up a ramp from the Bunker's second level that opened up into a motor pool building on the surface. To any outside observers, it would appear as though the trucks had been stored within the building and were leaving for a normal operation. The trucks themselves were standard U.S. Army two-and-a-half-ton diesel trucks—known within the military as a "deuce and a half," or simply a "deuce"—and the rear sections where the team and their gear were loaded were covered in fabric tarps in the same shade of olive drab as the trucks were painted. The small convoy moved briskly out of the main gate at Fort Wadsworth, then proceeded toward JFK airport.

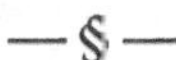

"Get that gear off the deuces and onto the plane!" shouted Captain Holton as the trucks came to a stop beside the enormous aircraft waiting on the tarmac. Now that the team was deploying into the field, they were all using their code names, and Holton was Captain Freedom.

Strongman looked up at the cargo plane. It was a C-5 Galaxy, the largest cargo plane in the Air Force inventory. It was at least sixty feet high, and its nose section had opened and was swung upward. The cockpit windows were visible at the top of the plane, in the shadow of the retracted nose, and a ramp led down to the ground from a cavernous interior.

Samson began loading the team's cargo, not with a forklift, but by lifting the pallet over his head and carrying it onto the waiting jet. Not to be outdone, and having no other assigned job beyond boarding the aircraft himself, Strongman hefted another of the waiting pallets from the back of the other deuce-and-a-half. Effortlessly, he held it above his head with a single hand, and walked up the ramp behind Samson.

The two men made quick work of loading the cargo, leaving Strongman holding only his personal bag, which contained a change of clothes, toiletries, and other personal items. When they had finished, Strongman climbed the spiral staircase—which was little more than a bare metal ladder in a spiral configuration—and entered the passenger compartment at the top of the aircraft, behind the cockpit. There was more than enough seating for the team, which numbered less than a dozen men, leaving them with entire rows of seats for each person. Although the seats reminded Strongman of an airliner, they instead faced toward the rear of the plane.

Strongman picked a row roughly in the middle of the passenger compartment, and threw his personal bag onto one of the seats. They were looking at nearly eight hours' flying time, and everyone seemed to be planning to use the spacious seating to lay down and sleep during the flight. His bag would make a decent makeshift pillow, Strongman decided.

One of the junior enlisted members of the team—who had joined after Strongman left the military, and been introduced to him as Airman First Class David Begay, *aka* War Eagle—climbed the stairs, a large box in his arms. War Eagle was Navajo, and had large wings growing from his back. While someone with flight powers wouldn't have been Strongman's first choice for the mission, War Eagle was brought along in a support role, as well as part of a second, contingency group that would remain on the surface in case of an attack on the Coast Guard cutter while the rest of the team was below the surface.

"I've got dinner!" War Eagle announced. "Boxed meals from the Air Force dining facility. Come get one, and hold onto it until you're hungry." The rest of the team made their way forward, and picked out a smaller container from the box that War Eagle carried. Looking inside, Strongman found a sandwich, a small bag of chips, and a can of Coke. *And here I thought the Air Force was supposed to eat better than the rest of us,* Strongman thought.

Everyone settled back into their seats, and the plane began to taxi onto the runway. Captain Freedom stood up in front of the seats. When he had everyone's attention, he said, "I spoke with command before we boarded. One of the Navy's new Deep Submergence Rescue Vehicles has been airlifted from San Diego, and will join us at the crash site.

Intelligence has also confirmed that the Red Legion has been deployed, and they're on a flight of their own as we speak. We're in a race, people. Let's make sure we win this one."

Captain Freedom took his seat, and everyone settled back in for the flight. The Red Legion was the Soviet Union's equivalent of Team Liberty: an elite team of military superhumans, ready to deploy on a moment's notice. The threat of an encounter had always been a possibility during the war, but had never come to pass when Strongman was still on the team. He hoped it stayed that way.

Chapter Two

The helicopter launched into the chilly Alaskan morning at Elmendorf Air Force Base, just northeast of Anchorage. A Sikorsky HH-52A "Seaguard," it was painted white with a bright red nose, tail, and diagonal red and blue stripes just before the tail boom—the hallmark paint scheme of the United States Coast Guard. As the helicopter reached the proper altitude, it turned to the southwest and accelerated forward, its nose dipping slightly.

After two and a half hours, the helicopter touched down at U.S. Coast Guard Base Kodiak, located on the north end of Kodiak Island. The Seaguard's maximum range was more than one hundred miles short of the crash site, necessitating a stopover for refueling. Given the necessity for speed, a "hot refueling" was undertaken. The helicopter's main engine continued to run while the ground crew rushed forward in protective gear and with firefighting gear at the ready. They quickly hooked up the refueling nozzle to the helicopter, and aviation fuel began to pour into the Seaguard's tank at fifty gallons per minute.

When refueling was complete, the ground crew secured the tank and cleared the pad, and the helicopter was airborne once again less than half an hour after landing. The Seaguard passed over Katmai National Park, then it was over the Bering Sea. Another four hours passed with nothing but the occasional fishing boat visible on the frigid ocean surface before a Coast Guard cutter came into view in the distance.

The Seaguard touched down on the helicopter landing pad at the aft end of the ship, and Strongman could see the number 723 painted in black on the white ship's hull. As he joined the rest of the team in exiting the helicopter, Strongman joined Samson in once again moving their pallets of equipment as several sailors gaped, eyes wide, from across the deck. Once they were satisfied that the gear was secure, Strongman and Samson joined the rest of the team as they were escorted to a compartment in the forward section of the ship.

"Welcome aboard the *Rush*," said a man waiting for them inside the compartment, which was clearly a briefing room and was dominated by a rectangular table surrounded by several chairs. He was wearing a dark blue uniform jacket and pants with a white shirt and black tie. It bore gold buttons and his four gold rank stripes indicated that he held the rank of captain, and he wore several rows of ribbons on his jacket. "I'm Captain Norman Fernald." He indicated the seats at the table before him. "Take a seat and I'll bring you up to speed on what's been going on the last few hours."

The members of the team all took their seats around the table as instructed. "The Air Force has a flight of F-4s on patrol," Fernald began, "and we have reports of a Russian Foxtrot-class submarine on course for our location. The U.S.S. *Seawolf* came alongside us an hour ago with the DSRV, so as soon as your team is ready, we can have a skiff transfer you over to the *Seawolf.*"

"Part of our team," Captain Freedom said, leaning forward in his chair and looking at Captain Fernald, "will remain on the *Rush* to provide combat air support." He indicated each member of the team as he introduced them. "Airman First Class Begay—War Eagle," the young Navajo man nodded, "Master Sergeant O'Dowd—Meteor," the dark-haired Army veteran nodded, "and Senior Master Sergeant Knapp—Blue Flame," the Air Force veteran also nodded, "have flight and offensive capabilities that are better suited on the surface." Blue Flame, like Strongman and Samson, was a veteran of the original incarnation of Team Liberty, twenty years earlier, while Meteor joined the team less than a year later.

Fernald nodded. "Thank you, captain. Let's hope we won't need them."

— § —

Strongman clambered out of the skiff and onto the deck of the submarine U.S.S. *Seawolf*. The submarine had surfaced near the U.S.C.G.C.

Rush just before the team boarded the skiff, and the deck in front of the conning tower was dominated by a miniature submarine that was attached to the deck. The conning tower itself bore the numbers 575 in large, white numbers, which stood in sharp contrast to the dark gray paint of the *Seawolf's* hull, which camouflaged the ship against the dark ocean waters.

The Deep Submergence Rescue Vehicle, or DSRV, was smaller and simpler than Strongman had expected. He had anticipated something more out of the *Thunderbirds* than what lay before him. It was a fairly plain cylinder painted green with a large, white engine propeller at the rear, and a small, orange dome at the top. It was mounted to the *Seawolf* by a pair of brackets at each end, and a white half-dome connected the bottom of the DSRV to the mother submarine.

This time around, Strongman and Samson didn't have to carry pallets of gear, which had since been distributed throughout the team's members, and much of it remained with the surface team on the *Rush*. Strongman felt even more conspicuous than usual in the primary colors of his superhero costume, which contrasted against the dark hull of the submarine and the dark uniforms of the sailors and soldiers around him. As they were ushered toward an open hatch at the rear of the submarine, Strongman fell in line behind the other members of the team, all of whom were clad in wet suits. Every member of the team, including Strongman, was armed with a Colt M1911A1 semi-automatic pistol and an assortment of grenades, but several members carried other weapons as well.

Captain Freedom led the team, a CAR-15 slung over his shoulder. The CAR-15 XM177 was a carbine variant of the M-16A1 rifle used by the U.S. military. Captain Freedom had enhanced strength, but his most tactically useful power was an ability to teleport short distances. Behind him was Samson, the senior enlisted member of Team Liberty. Samson, like Strongman, had superstrength, but while Strongman carried a minimal firearms loadout that freed up his hands, Samson carried a massive M60 machine gun.

Samson was followed by Typhoon, another veteran of the original Team Liberty roster. Typhoon—Senior Chief Petty Officer Tom Sanders—had the ability to breathe underwater, which could be invaluable on a mission like this. He carried a standard M-16A1 over his shoulder.

Behind Typhoon was Ferro—Marine Master Sergeant Lawrence Nichols—whose skin had permanently turned from its original dark brown color to a dark, steel-gray color. His metallic skin proved virtually impenetrable, yet still just as flexible as regular skin, a fact that perplexed the scientists who studied the team members and their abilities. Ferro carried an M-16A1, which was also outfitted with an M203 grenade launcher.

Rounding out the team was Brainpunch—Army Sergeant First Class Luis Marquez—who possessed powerful telekinetic abilities, and he carried an Uzi submachine gun. Strongman had served with Ferro and Brainpunch during his return to Team Liberty during the Vietnam War, and was glad to see they had both been promoted in the intervening years.

One by one, the team descended through the hatch and into the *Seawolf*. Once aboard, they were escorted to the ship's bridge. Klaxons sounded and Strongman felt the ship's deck begin to angle as the ship dove beneath the surface. At the center of the room, a man in a khaki uniform turned around to face them. Strongman immediately noticed the rank insignia on the man's collar: silver oak leaves.

"Welcome aboard," the man said, extending a hand to Captain Freedom. "I'm Commander John Webster, commanding officer of the *Seawolf*." Captain Freedom took the man's hand and shook it firmly. "We're already underway and should be at depth to release the DSRV in about thirty minutes." He raised a hand to indicate the noncommissioned officer who had escorted the team from the hatch to the bridge. "The chief here will show you to the forward hatch so you can get ready to move."

Captain Freedom nodded. "Thank you, sir," he said. Webster nodded, then turned and resumed his duties in overseeing the ship's safe dive to a depth of just over 300 meters. The chief petty officer indicated with a wave of his hand for the team to follow him. They made their way through several hatches leading away from the bridge, and soon found themselves at the forward hatch. It struck Strongman that these sailors all coexisted within the tight confines of this submarine, which sometimes didn't surface for months at a time.

The chief opened the hatch above their heads, and they filed individually into the waiting DSRV. They found themselves inside a spherical compartment within the small submarine, and a pair of hatches led to the front and the back of the craft. Upon reflection, it made sense to Strongman that it would be designed this way, so any section that was compromised at the extreme depths the ship traveled to would not flood the entire vessel.

The forward hatch opened, and Strongman saw a cramped control cockpit with two sailors inside. One of them stood at the hatch, and spoke briefly with Captain Freedom. When their conversation ended, he returned to the control compartment and sealed the hatch behind him.

"Make yourselves comfortable," Captain Freedom announced. "Once we're at depth, the pilots will take us to the crash site and attach us to the spacecraft. We'll have to cut through the hull to make our entry, and they'll remain on station until we leave."

— § —

The dark-haired sailor, one of the two men who had piloted the DSRV, extinguished the blowtorch in his hand and stepped back from the hatch. Ferro moved forward, then drove his boot onto the exposed hull of the alien spacecraft. It shot down into the ship, and clanged loudly against the deck below a moment later. Ferro readied his M-16, then dropped through the hatch.

Strongman followed a moment later, his pistol in his hand. The corridor that he landed in was dim, lit only by what he assumed must be emergency lighting. The surfaces were all made from the same brushed silvery metal that made up the hull of the ship, which actually helped reflect the minimal light.

One by one, the members of Team Liberty boarded the alien ship, beginning with the strongest and most durable members first. As each set of boots hit the deck, their owner stepped forward, weapon ready, to clear the entryway and provide cover for their teammates as they followed. There was a soft rush of displaced air as Captain Freedom teleported down from the hatch.

Silently, the team began to make their way into the ship. Ferro and Samson took point, their invulnerable hides shielding their more vulnerable teammates, while Strongman took up the rear, in case of attack from behind. Not for the first time, Strongman found himself wishing that his former teammate, Danny Barr, who had the codename Lucky-man, was still with the team, but the man's ability to subconsciously manipulate probabilities—effectively giving him and anyone in his immediate vicinity the power of "good luck"—worked in his favor to prevent his being drafted back into the military when the Vietnam War escalated in the late 1960s.

Gunfire from the front of the group snapped Strongman's full attention back to the situation at hand. He had been walking backward, keeping his gaze on the corridor behind them, and turned his head quickly toward the sound of the firefight. Like the others, Strongman dropped to a kneeling stance along the wall. He could see several indistinct shapes moving at the intersection of this corridor with another about a dozen yards away. Ferro adjusted his M-16, and pulled the trigger on the M203 grenade launcher.

A deafening explosion shook the deck, and smoke filled the intersection of the corridors. Before it could clear, two figures shot out of the cloud, arms extended as impossibly long legs that resembled the hind legs of a giant lizard propelled them toward the team at an unbelievable pace. Within moments, the team found themselves locked in close-quarters combat with what could only be described as giant lizard men, identical to the photographs they'd seen in the briefing but far faster than Strongman had believed possible.

Two more of the aliens rushed out from an intersection that the team had passed just before the attack began, clearly hoping to flank them. They wore helmets with large, slanted eye-shaped lenses, but no apparent armor of any kind—just a sheer, tight, jumpsuit. Strongman opened fire with his pistol, and one of the two dropped to the deck like a puppet with its strings cut. The other leaped onto him and bit down on his forearm. Had the alien done this to one of the other team members nearby, that could have reduced the arm to a gory stump just below the elbow, but instead, the crocodile-like skin around the alien's mouth pulled back in a clear expression of surprise and pain.

The alien released its grip on his arm, and Strongman slammed a fist into its helmeted head. Against a human opponent, he would typically pull his punches, but against these creatures, he felt no such compulsion. The alien's helmet folded inward like an empty aluminum can, and gore splattered as its skull imploded within. A detached part of him noted that the blood on his fist was the same shade of red as a human's.

Strongman looked up to assess his surroundings as the sounds of fighting began to fade. Every member of the team traded glances, confirming they were uninjured. The team re-formed at the center of the corridor, and proceeded cautiously forward. No one spoke, with Captain Freedom and Ferro using hand signals to silently relay messages.

In addition to the two aliens that Strongman had killed, he saw the bodies of three more as he passed where the front of the group had been, and one more alien body in the corridor where Ferro's grenade had exploded, one side shredded to pulp by the fragmentation round, and the arm severed. He scanned all around the team's rear flank as they moved deeper into the ship, wary of further attack.

The team came to a halt nearly ten minutes later. They had explored a sizeable chunk of the ship without further incident, and were near what appeared to be a docking bay of some kind at the center. As Ferro and Samson flanked the doorway into the cavernous chamber and peered around the edges of the passageway, they could hear faint voices from within.

Those voices were speaking Russian.

Captain Freedom gave a series of hand signals, and the team silently filed through the doorway. They took cover wherever they could find it on the other side, and Strongman crouched next to Typhoon behind what seemed to be some kind of free-standing console several feet from the doorway. Captain Freedom teleported himself behind a support column several yards into the room, and they waited for his next signal.

"Russian soldiers," Captain Freedom called out, his CAR-15 at the ready but staying behind the cover of the support column. "This is Captain Freedom of Team Liberty. We have already taken control of this vessel, and your presence is not welcome. You are ordered to leave immediately. This is your only warning."

Silence greeted the Americans, and Typhoon exchanged a glance with Strongman. The moment was short lived, however, and the roar of small arms fire echoed throughout the bay. Typhoon pivoted to face the Russians, and brought his M-16 to bear, its muzzle perched atop the console.

"Of course they couldn't just leave," Typhoon muttered as he began to return fire. "Always gotta do things the hard way."

Strongman stood, bringing his pistol to bear in the direction of the Russian soldiers. He could see at least four of them, taking cover wherever they could find it. They were all dressed in wet suits, and had only what gear they could have carried across at a swim. The DSRV technology was still fairly new, Strongman remembered, and the Russians didn't have one of their own. They would have had to use a diving bell to get to the right depth before swimming over in wet suits.

He fired off several shots, but didn't actually hit any of the Russians. The gunfire prevented them from leaving their cover positions, however, which meant that none of them were likely to be invulnerable like him, Ferro, and Samson. Bullets ricocheted off of his body as he slowly began to walk toward the Russians. Strongman realized the trap had been sprung as soon as he stepped into it.

Two of the Russian soldiers popped up from their cover positions just long enough to throw something. An instant later, a pair of grenades landed at his feet. One spewed a thick cloud of smoke, obscuring everyone's view of the opposing side of the fight. The other exploded with a deafening noise and a flash of magnesium light.

Stars filled his vision and his ears rang. As he blinked in an attempt to clear his eyesight, Strongman felt the deck shake ever so subtly an instant before a fist connected with his jaw and sent him flying into the air. He crashed into one of the consoles, which crumpled like paper under the impact.

Hands grabbed him at his shoulders, and Strongman felt himself being dragged backward. His vision began to clear enough that he could make out the faces of Typhoon and Samson, but he couldn't understand what anyone was saying. The ringing sound was beginning to subside, but everything was muffled and dulled, like he was hearing everything underwater.

Moments later, they were back in the corridor outside the docking bay. Samson helped Strongman to his feet, and he brushed himself off. Strongman followed the group as they withdrew back into the ship. He fired his own pistol at the Russians whenever it seemed like he had a halfway decent shot, but if he was actually hitting anything, he couldn't tell.

"That went well," Strongman muttered as the team regrouped further down the corridor. He shook his head and berated himself, "I walked right into that like an idiot. Of course they'd be ready for someone like me. They've gotta know as much about us as we do about them."

"They won't be able to pull that trick twice," Captain Freedom said. "We need to secure our control of the ship. Samson and Typhoon, you're with me; we're going to take the ship's control room. Strongman, Ferro, and Brainpunch, you're on the engineering section." Heads nodded with serious expressions as everyone acknowledged their orders. "Let's do this."

Chapter Three

Strongman could hear the distant sound of gunfire as Captain Freedom's team moved further down the corridor toward the ship's control room. They had succeeded in getting the Russians to split up as well, with one group pursuing them and the other following Strongman's team.

The teams seemed to be evenly matched, with three of the Russians hot on their heels. He recognized them from the briefing materials he'd been given to review on the plane. At least one of them actually was invulnerable to gunfire, because Strongman was certain that at least one of the rounds he'd fired from his pistol had hit the man. The Russian lived up to his code name, Medved, which meant "bear," and the thickly-mustachioed Russian kept coming, giving no indication that he'd been shot.

The second Russian was thin and wiry, and easily dodged anything thrown or shot in his direction. He was called Drekavac, after a creature in Slavic folklore—a name that literally translated to "the screamer." The final member of the Russian team was a thin woman with long, claw-like fingers, who loped along on all fours like a wild creature, and caromed off the walls of the corridor with ease. She was called Strzyga, after a vampire-like creature from Slavic mythology, and was reportedly the Red Legion's second-in-command.

The trio of Russians was gaining on them quickly, and their gunfire was having no effect. As he passed through an archway in the corridor behind Ferro and Brainpunch, Strongman noticed a control panel of some sort on the wall beside the arch. He took aim and fired, and the panel exploded from the bullet's impact. An instant later, a pair of enormous doors slid shut in the archway, blocking the Russians' path.

He'd bought them some breathing room, but that wouldn't stop the Russians forever. As he turned and urged his teammates to run faster, he saw that one of the doors was already beginning to warp under Medved's relentless assault. Strongman could hear powerful blows against the metal of what he guessed must be blast doors of some kind. It made sense that, when damaged, the doors would close automatically; that would prevent the total loss of atmosphere if the ship suffered a hull breach in space. That none had closed when they breached the hull with the DSRV must mean that they weren't triggered automatically unless the ship detected a change in atmospheric pressure.

The three Americans rounded a corner at an intersection of two corridors. They were very near to where their briefing materials said that the ship's engineering section would be located when the pounding of Medved's fists against the blast door stopped, followed a moment later by the screech of rending metal. The Russians would be through the door in a matter of seconds. As soon as they crossed the threshold into the engineering section, Strongman began to search for a way to seal the doors.

A muttered curse drew his attention, and out of the corner of his eye, Strongman saw Ferro bring his M-16 to bear on something behind him. He turned and, to his surprise, saw that some of the aliens had survived their initial assault on the ship. There were four of the lanky, green lizard-like creatures standing at a console at the center of the room. Whatever they had been doing, they had stopped and were looking, equally surprised, at the three humans who had just burst into the room.

The Saurians' surprise was short lived, however, and three of the four leaped toward the Americans. Their legs had joints much like a chicken, Strongman realized, and the three soared through the air with a speed and grace that he hadn't expected. Brainpunch fired off a burst from his Uzi, but the bullets missed the alien streaking toward him. An instant later, Ferro shattered the plastic stock of his M-16 when he used it as a club against the jaw of the Saurian attacking him.

Strongman's attention was quickly drawn to the Saurian attacking him, however, as it landed on his chest, knocking him to the deck with a resounding thud. The pistol in his hand went flying as he hit the floor, but it would have been of limited use for him at close range anyhow. The alien lunged its head at him, and his vision filled with an enormous mouth filled with razor-sharp teeth. An instant before those jaws could close on his head, he swung his arm into the path of the bite. The Saurian bit down on Strongman's forearm, then recoiled almost immediately. Blood flowed down his arm.

The Saurian staggered back, its hands flying to its mouth, and it screeched an unmistakable cry of pain. Strongman inspected his arm, and found several of the creature's razor-sharp teeth imbedded in the now-bloody glove. He pulled one out, and saw that his skin hadn't even been broken in the attack.

Anger burning in its eyes, the alien rounded on him once again. It crouched, spreading its arms, and held the claws on its hands menacingly open. The alien leaped forward, and just as it came near, Strongman let loose with a powerful blow. His fist caught the alien across its wounded jaw, then carried it downward. Continuing the punch, Strongman drove the alien's head into the deck. He could hear the sound of its bones snapping, and it slumped to the deck, unconscious.

An all-too-human scream tore Strongman's attention from the still form of the Saurian before him. The alien that had attacked Brainpunch had him pinned to the ground, and its teeth were sunk deep into the point where his neck and shoulder met. Blood sprayed from the wound and the Saurian shook its head, causing its teeth to rend the man's flesh further still.

Strongman leaped toward the Saurian, and struck it dead center with incredible force. He carried the creature through the air for several feet before they hit the deck and tumbled for another couple of yards. The alien slashed at him with its claws, but succeeded only in tearing the reinforced cloth of his tunic before they rolled to a stop. Strongman pinned the Saurian under his knees, then held its throat with his left hand. He drew back his right fist, then drove it into the lizard-like being's head. The skull shattered like a watermelon under the blow, spraying blood and viscera in all directions as the deck trembled beneath them.

He stood, wiping the gore from his fist on the dead alien's clothing. He turned, then jogged quickly back to Brainpunch's side. The man had an enormous chunk of flesh taken from his shoulder, and lay in an expanding pool of blood. His eyes remained open, unblinking and unseeing. Strongman muttered a curse, then turned to see how Ferro was holding up in his own fight.

The Russians picked that moment to enter the engineering section. They came to a sudden halt, their shock at seeing the aliens plainly evident on their faces. The Saurian that had been grappling with Ferro had apparently had about as much luck in its fight as the one that had attacked Strongman, and Ferro hit it with a backhand across the face that sent it sprawling. It bowled into Strzyga, and the pair went down in a tangle of arms and legs.

The two were evenly matched, both striking out with fists, feet, and claws. Strzyga rolled onto her back as the alien leaped toward her, and lashed out with a kick with both legs that sent the creature flying into Medved's waiting grasp. He enveloped the Saurian in a bear hug, his grasp tightening by the moment as the alien writhed and screeched. Strongman heard the alien's bones begin to break, and within seconds it ceased struggling and its head fell limply to its chest. Medved released his grip, and the alien dropped to the floor. Its face slammed into the deck, but it didn't react or move any further.

The last remaining Saurian dove behind the console, then came back up a moment later. It had an object of some kind in its hands—long, metallic, boxy. It lifted the object in an all-too-familiar manner, holding a handle in one hand, supporting the front with its other, and bringing it near to its face. The alien had a rifle of some kind, and it was aiming it at them.

A deafening shriek filled the room, and the Saurian was knocked from its feet. Strongman clamped his hands over his ears, and he could see that Drekavac was standing nearby with his mouth wide in a shout—the reason for his codename was obvious. Moments later, the scream—which delivered a kinetic blow to the alien as well as the acoustic assault—stopped.

Strongman's ears were ringing as he removed his hands from them. Everyone present had been deafened by the cacophonous attack, save for Drekavac himself. Ferro was on his hands and knees, shaking his head in a vain attempt to restore his hearing. Medved and Strzyga had collapsed to the deck, blood trickling from their ears. The Saurian slowly picked itself up from the floor, and stumbled woozily toward a nearby hatch.

Strongman attempted to give chase, but his own equilibrium had been affected by Drekavac's sonic attack. After the first step, his run turned into a stumble, and he tripped over his own feet. He fell to his knees, breaking his fall with his hand as the room spun around him.

Sound began to return a few moments later, with the shriek of the ship's alarm klaxon emerging slowly from the ringing that had filled his world. The klaxon grew steadily louder with each repetition, though everything beyond the ringing still sounded like he was underwater.

The deck heaved under him. For a moment, Strongman thought that his equilibrium was continuing to fail, but the lights flickered an instant later. The room was plunged into darkness for a moment, and when the lights came back on, they were only at a fraction of their previous intensity.

Just as he had managed to rise to his feet once again, the deck pitched once more. A deep, rending sound filled the ship, and when the ship stopped moving once again, the deck had settled at an angle. Ferro looked quickly at him with alarm evident on his face.

Strongman grasped Ferro's outstretched hand and helped his teammate to his feet. The deck had largely stopped moving, but he could still feel a slight tremor beneath his feet. The two rounded on the trio of Russians, hoping they'd be smart enough to stop fighting with them until the immediate threat to both groups had passed.

The sound of gunfire echoed from the corridor beyond the entry to the engineering compartment. Between bursts of semiautomatic rounds that sounded like M-16s and AK-47s, Strongman could also discern the steady thump of the high-caliber rounds from an M-60 machine gun. The rest of both teams must be nearby, and were still actively shooting at one another.

The sounds of the gunfire drew steadily closer, and Strongman glanced at Medved. The burly Russian was helping Strzyga to her feet. After a moment, Medved realized that someone was looking at him, and he quickly locked eyes with Strongman. Their faces were both tight and serious, and Medved nodded curtly.

Three men ran into the room a moment later, weapons up as their gazes darted around the room, taking in their surroundings. Samson remained facing the door, his M-60 at the ready. Captain Freedom and Typhoon aimed their rifles at the trio of Russians, while Captain Freedom acknowledged Strongman with a nod.

"Don't move!" Captain Freedom barked at the Russians. Medved slowly spread his hands at his sides, indicating that he was offering no resistance.

"Sir," Strongman began, loudly enough to get Captain Freedom's attention without resorting to yelling. "We've got bigger problems." Captain Freedom turned his head to shoot a questioning glance at Strongman, while Typhoon remained focused on the Russians.

Samson chose that moment to open fire with his M-60. In the confined space, the sound was nearly as deafening as Drekavac's sonic attack had been a few minutes earlier. Strongman turned his attention to see what was happening, and saw the members of the other group of Russians diving for whatever cover they could find.

"We need a cease fire," Strongman said to Captain Freedom between the bursts of high-caliber weapons fire. He quickly summarized what had happened before the rest of Team Liberty had joined them in the engineering compartment. "You can feel it in the deck, sir," Strongman said. "The ship's starting to slide. It's only a matter of time before it either falls off the edge and into deeper water and gets crushed by the pressure, or it blows up, because I'm pretty sure the alien that got away set some kind of self destruct before he high-tailed it out of here."

Chapter Four

D ammit," Captain Freedom muttered, shaking his head. He returned his attention to the three Russians in front of him. "Any of you speak English?"

"Da," Strzyga said, nodding as she continued to hold her hands up at her sides. "A little. Is not best language."

"Good enough," Captain Freedom replied. "I'm going to order my men to cease fire. I want you to explain what's going on to your people. Will you do that?"

"Da," Strzyga replied.

"Cease fire!" Captain Freedom called out. Samson removed his finger from the trigger of his M-60 and allowed the barrel to drop toward the deck. Captain Freedom looked to Strzyga and said, "You're up."

The thin Russian woman stepped forward and called out in her native language. A man's voice replied from the corridor. Strzyga continued toward the compartment's doorway, and three more members of the Red Legion stepped out from their cover positions and approached her as they spoke with one another. They met at the threshold of the doorway, and continued to speak for nearly two minutes. Finally, the man, whom Strongman guessed must be the team's leader for this mission, nodded seriously, his lips pressed into a thin line. The group turned and walked back toward Captain Freedom.

"Captain Freedom," Strzyga said, trying but failing to hide her disdain for the codename while saying it, "this is commanding officer,

Polkovnik Zashchitnik." She paused, then translated the Russian term, "Colonel Defender." She then spoke briefly with her superior in Russian, and he clearly didn't like what he was hearing.

"Colonel Defender," Strzyga translated uncomfortably, "does not believe situation as," she paused, uncertain in her choice of words, "as bad as he is told."

"I don't care if he believes it," Captain Freedom said. "This ship is about to be destroyed, one way or another. It's about to drop off this cliff, a half mile down, and the pressure will crush it, if the self destruct doesn't blow it up first. We're leaving. Go, stay, I don't care. I'm just asking you not to shoot us in the back while we go."

As if to punctuate his comments, the deck shuddered once again, and the ship moved along the ocean floor, nearly knocking them all off of their feet. Strzyga translated Captain Freedom's words into Russian, and Strongman could tell that she was also pleading with her commanding officer to see reason. The colonel was clearly unmoved, and shook his head before speaking.

Strzyga's mouth dropped. She turned to Captain Freedom, and said, "He say Russians can fix ship. We not leaving, and you prisoners."

"Like hell," Captain Freedom spat an instant before punching Colonel Defender in the jaw. The burly Russian rolled with the blow, then straightened. A toothy grin spread across his face and he said something in Russian. He shot a fist at Captain Freedom, who vanished with a muffled popping sound a heartbeat before the blow landed, reappearing just as quickly beside Ferro, several yards away.

The room instantly erupted into chaos. Both teams began fighting, and the deck continued to shudder as the ship continued its inexorable slide toward the abyss. Medved launched himself at Strongman, while Strzyga turned to leap toward Typhoon. Colonel Defender continued to chase after Captain Freedom, who repeatedly teleported away an instant before the Russian could reach him. Ferro attacked Drekavac, hoping to render the lanky Russian unconscious before he could use his sonic attack to incapacitate the American team. The remaining two Russian soldiers, whom Strongman didn't recognize, pounced on Samson.

Medved tried to wrap his arms around Strongman's torso and place him in one of his signature bear hugs, but Strongman had anticipated that. He raised his forearms just before the burly Russian grabbed hold of him, and used that leverage and his own superstrength to force Medved's arms open. Free of the Russian's grip, Strongman threw a haymaker at the man's jaw, but Medved caught it at the last moment.

Drekavac inhaled deeply as Ferro ran toward him. Just as he was about to release one of his powerful and deafening screams, Ferro clobbered him with a metallic fist. The force of the blow knocked Drekavac to the deck, and Ferro was upon him in an instant. Straddling the prone Russian, Ferro laced the fingers of his hands together, then brought them down on the smaller man's head. Drekavac went limp, knocked into unconsciousness. With Drekavac down, Ferro bounded away to help Samson.

Colonel Defender bellowed something in Russian as he again charged futilely after Captain Freedom, who teleported away once more at the last moment. The Russian officer slammed into a wall at a run, leaving a large dent where his fists impacted the area where his American counterpart's head had been a moment earlier. Captain Freedom appeared a heartbeat later near the console that the alien had been using during Strongman's team's assault on the engineering compartment less than twenty minutes earlier. As Colonel Defender swept his gaze around the room to find where his American prey had vanished to this time, Captain Freedom grabbed the alien's fallen rifle, which lay on the deck inches away from his booted feet.

With a roar of anger and frustration, Colonel Defender charged once again at Captain Freedom, now on the other side of the engineering compartment. After a moment to take stock of the weapon in his hands, the American officer hefted the rifle into a firing position and took aim. Either blinded by rage or confident of his own indestructibility, Colonel Defender ignored the weapon and continued to run, his legs pistoning powerfully against the deck.

Captain Freedom pulled the trigger of the alien weapon, and a burst of energy shot forth from the rifle's barrel. There was almost no recoil, and he watched in astonishment as the blast struck Colonel Defender squarely in the center of his chest. It knocked the Russian officer off of his feet, not only halting his forward momentum, but driving him back several feet. He slammed onto his back, the deck reverberating with the impact. A wisp of smoke rose from the point of impact on the Russian's uniform coat.

The fighting quickly stopped as the Russians all paused to stare in astonishment at their fallen commanding officer. Strzyga wriggled in Typhoon's grasp, breaking free and kicking her feet off of his chest. She bounded away from him as he fell to his backside, and within moments she was at Colonel Defender's side. She quickly checked his pulse and placed an ear by his mouth. She said something in Russian.

"He still alive," she repeated in her broken English.

"Tough sonofabitch," Strongman muttered.

"We stop fighting," Strzyga announced, then repeated herself in Russian. "Comrade Colonel mistaken. Is much danger here. Go. We must leave before is too late." She turned and began to address the other members of her team in their native language.

Captain Freedom nodded and turned to face his own team. "Strongman," he began, "take Brainpunch. Ferro, secure the prisoner." He indicated the lone remaining alien, still unconscious from the beating it received at Strongman's hands. "We're getting out of here."

$$-\S-$$

The dark-haired sailor aboard the Deep Submergence Rescue Vehicle stepped back in alarm as Ferro carried the unconscious alien prisoner up the ladder and through the hatch. Ferro lifted the reptilian creature off of his shoulder and set it down, propping it into a seated position against a nearby bulkhead. He and Samson proceeded to stand watch over the unconscious alien, its hands and feet bound with olive drab colored nylon 550 parachute cord.

At the center of the small compartment, the dark-haired sailor dogged the hatch connecting the rescue submarine to the hull of the alien spacecraft, barely taking his eyes off the prisoner the whole time, the color drained from his face.

"We caught sight of something," the sailor said to Captain Freedom, struggling to maintain his composure, "just before your team came back aboard. Some kind of smaller craft shot out of the ship, then headed toward the surface. It was fast, too. Wish I knew how they compensate for that kind of rapid pressure change. No way we could surface that quickly without giving everyone the bends."

"Must have been that alien survivor," Strongman said. He was only a couple of feet away, helping to secure the team's gear, and couldn't help but overhear the conversation. "Some kind of escape pod."

Captain Freedom nodded in agreement. "Nothing we can do about that," he said. "Any sign of the Russian team?"

"Not before I came back here to help you all aboard, sir," the sailor said. "They don't have DSRVs, so they'd have to get back into their diving gear in order to swim to their diving bell. We finally spotted that about twenty minutes ago, and we've been keeping an eye on it."

"Understood," Captain Freedom said. The DSRV rocked as the spacecraft shifted once more, edging closer still to the chasm below. "Thank you, sailor. Let's get the hell out of here before that ship drags us all down with it."

"Aye, sir," the sailor said. He nodded to Captain Freedom, then returned to the forward compartment with his copilot, shutting the hatch behind him.

"All hands," the tinny voice of the second sailor crackled over the speakers mounted inside the DSRV, "secure for undocking." A moment later, the soft sound of the clamps holding the rescue submarine in place against the alien ship's hull echoed inside the cabin. The deck shifted slightly, swaying from side to side as the DSRV maneuvered free of the larger vessel. "We're clear," the sailor's voice said a moment later. "Returning to *Seawolf.*"

The alien captive picked that moment to regain consciousness. Its head snapped from side to side, frantically taking in its surroundings. It struggled against its bonds, arms and legs thrashing futilely in place. Samson hefted his M-60 machine gun, and leveled it inches away from the alien's face. It immediately stopped moving, its gaze fixed, wide-eyed, on the tip of the barrel. Samson sneered at the alien.

"We're picking up multiple contacts," the dark-haired sailor's voice issued from the speaker overhead. "Looks like the Russians are heading back for their diving bell."

"The ship is beginning to list," the other sailor added. "Won't be long now." A low groaning sound made its way through the DSRV's hull, punctuating the sailor's words. "Approaching *Seawolf.* Prepare for docking."

"Welcome aboard," Commander Webster greeted them as Captain Freedom, Samson, and Strongman were escorted onto the *Seawolf's* bridge. The rest of the team was securing their prisoner in the cramped ship's brig. Most of the crew wasn't even aware of what was going on, believing it to be a surprise submarine rescue exercise. Keeping the alien out of sight was just as important as keeping it restrained. "Sonar shows the ship is beginning to slide off the edge of the cliff."

"One of them set a self destruct device," Captain Freedom said. "We don't know how long until it goes off."

"Helm, put some distance between us," Webster ordered, turning his head to address the sailors seated at the pair of steering wheels in front of him.

"Contact is beginning to descend," the sonar operator announced. "It's falling now, sir." A moment later, he added, "I'm picking up an implosion, sir."

Commander Webster nodded. "Prepare to surface. Let's get our guests home."

Within an hour, Strongman was seated in a skiff, across from the alien prisoner, who was flanked by Ferro and Samson. The alien was concealed by a wool blanket, and the makeshift rope bindings had been replaced by steel handcuffs and leg restraints. Brainpunch's body lay in a body bag from the *Seawolf's* morgue, and Typhoon kept watch over their fallen teammate.

The ride from the *Seawolf* to the *Rush* was brief, and within minutes, they were unloading their gear, their prisoner, and their dead aboard the Coast Guard cutter. With the help of their teammates who had remained on the surface, they loaded everything aboard their waiting helicopter. Captain Freedom gave a short briefing to Captain Fernald, and the team boarded the helicopter.

The flight back to Elmendorf Air Force Base was somber. A few people shared stories about their time with Brainpunch. Tears were shed, along with a few muted laughs. Losing a teammate was never easy. Over the years, Strongman had lost many of them, from his time in Korea during that war, to his friend Nucleus less than a decade earlier, before he returned to the military and Team Liberty in Vietnam.

Strongman fell asleep shortly after the helicopter left Coast Guard Base Kodiak. It had been a long, exhausting day, both physically and, particularly, mentally. He woke as the helicopter bounced, its wheels settling on the pavement of the flightline at Elmendorf.

A deuce and a half waited for them, and everyone quickly transferred everything from the helicopter to the truck. Captain Freedom had not been idle during the trip back, as a Security Forces escort was ready and waiting to take the prisoner into custody. Another vehicle was waiting to take Brainpunch's body to the base's morgue, where it would be kept until the team returned to New York.

The deuce took them to the base's temporary lodging facilities. They unloaded their gear and checked in at the front desk. True to the Air Force's reputation, this was like a hotel in the civilian world. While not a four-star resort, it was easily the equal of a typical hotel, down to the furnishings.

Strongman tossed his bag with his personal items on the end of the bed. He stripped off his costume, which was still stained with the blood of the alien he had killed, and took a long, hot shower.

Chapter Five

Strongman's sleep had been anything but restful. His mind had presented him with a string of nightmares, recounting the worst case scenarios for every way the mission could have gone badly, to memories of past traumas. The worst was reliving the day he'd been asked to identify Nucleus' body in the morgue after he'd been murdered by the mob.

By the time he'd awoken yet again, it was nearly four in the morning, and he gave up on trying to get any further sleep. He took a spare costume out of his bag and laid it out on the end of the bed, then pulled out a pair of sweatpants and a t-shirt, along with a matching pair of athletic shoes. He dressed, then left to get in a run and, hopefully, clear his head.

It didn't take long for him to find the base running track, thanks to a map conveniently provided at the front desk. He jogged there in the pre-dawn darkness. When he finally reached the track, he saw that it was already in use by several dozen people. Apparently, one of the units on the base was doing their morning PT there.

He slipped in among the runners on the track. He took the outermost lane, which was sparsely populated, since most of the runners present were clustered toward the inner lanes. He focused on his breathing and on moving his feet and arms, and let everything else fall away around him.

After several minutes of running, Strongman began to notice that he'd been running at a faster pace than he'd intended. Much faster.

While he didn't have superspeed, due to his superstrength, he could propel himself much farther and faster than a baseline human. Without realizing he had done so, he'd been running at a pace somewhere around thirty miles per hour, and everyone at the track was now stopped and watching him with wide-eyed fascination.

Strongman slowed to a stop near the entrance to the track. As he did, one of the Air Force personnel gathered nearby began walking over to him.

"God *damn* do you run fast, sir," the man said. "I don't think I've ever seen you here before. What unit you with?"

"Team Liberty," Strongman said. "Just passing through. Needed to get a run in to clear my head."

"Team... Team Liberty?" the man asked, floored. "Here?"

"Just passing through," Strongman repeated. "Don't spread it around, though. OPSEC." The man nodded vigorously at the acronym, which stood for Operational Security. The need to maintain secrecy about unit movements and activities was well understood in the military, inspiring turns of phrase like the adage that "loose lips sink ships" in the Second World War.

"Understood, sir," the man said. "It's an honor to meet you. You do look familiar, though."

Strongman chuckled. "I'm Strongman. It's just less obvious without the costume. Got recalled for this last op, but I'm on my way home now."

The man's eyes widened once more. He extended a hand, and Strongman shook it. "It's an honor, sir," the man repeated as they shook hands. The others, seeing the interaction, began to walk over as well. Within moments, Strongman was surrounded by a throng of admirers, all beside themselves to meet one of the world's first superheroes.

He chatted with the group for a few minutes, answering their questions, and shaking their hands. Soon, they all departed, explaining that they had to get back to their dormitory to shower and change, so as not to be late to work for the day. Once they were gone, Strongman began to run laps once again, focusing on his breathing and the motion of his body, letting his mind go blank. He ran until the sun began to rise.

He jogged back to the base lodging facility. As he entered the lobby on his way back to his room, he glanced at the clock mounted on the wall behind the front desk. It read 4:45. The team wouldn't be gathering for their flight back to New York until eight a.m. He still had several hours to spare, so after taking his morning shower, he took his time getting dressed and repacking the bag of his personal belongings.

At six, he joined several of the other members of the team as they gathered in the lobby. Together, they walked to the nearby dining facility, where they got breakfast. The Air Force dining facility was set up cafeteria style, and each of them took a tray, then proceeded down the line and collected their food from the airmen working the line.

The rest of the team was all dressed in standard OG-107 olive drab uniforms, blending in with the rest of the military personnel on base, even with variations on branch and name patches. The Air Force personnel all wore blue tags with white letters, and their rank insignia was in similar colors on their sleeves. The Army had white tags with black lettering for the names over the right pocket, and black tags with yellow "U.S. ARMY" lettering over the left, and the gold-on-black rank stripes were sewn onto their sleeves in the same manner as the Air Force. The Marines wore no name tags, and the Marine Corps seal was silkscreened onto the left pocket. They wore similar rank stripes as the Army, albeit with a red background color. While the Navy senior enlisted personnel typically wore a khaki uniform, the Navy members of Team Liberty wore the olive drab uniforms as well; they featured olive drab tags with black lettering, and their black rank insignia were sewn onto their collars.

Strongman, however, was the only member of the team not currently serving in the military. He wore not a military uniform, but his superhero costume. The airmen working in the dining facility joined those seated at nearby tables and eating their breakfasts in staring, open mouthed, at one of the most famous superheroes on the planet. The young men working on the other side of the serving line took twice as long for his meal because they paid more attention to him than to the food they were dishing out.

At the end of the line was a cash register. Samson identified himself and the group to the airman at the register, and he pulled out a clipboard with a pen attached to it on a chain. Each member of the team took turns filling out the form on the clipboard. When Strongman approached the register, he took the clipboard from the gawking young man with a pair of stripes denoting an Airman First Class. He found the first blank line on the form, then filled out his information for the accounting people to bill the cost of the meals to Team Liberty. He handed the clipboard back, flashing an amused grin at the starstruck young man.

The team gathered together at a pair of tables at the center of the dining room. They ate quietly, and any conversation, while muted, was kept to nondescript topics. Due to operational security, they knew not to discuss anything related to their mission, or even something as seemingly innocuous as when they were expected to meet up to board their flight back to New York that morning. Even here on a secured military base, there was always the nagging thought in the back of their minds that *someone* could be listening in, and none wanted to risk their lips being the ones that sunk their proverbial ship.

Strongman dug in to his meal. The food here was miles ahead of anything he'd ever gotten when he had served in the Army during the Korean War. His plate was piled high with bacon, eggs, hashbrowns, a couple of sausage links, and glasses of orange juice and water. True, he'd eaten better outside of the military world, but the Air Force really did provide a high quality of life standard for its people compared to the other branches, from what he'd seen during his lifetime.

After the team had finished their breakfast, they again moved as a group back to the lodging facility. When they had all gathered in the lobby, Samson glanced around to ensure that no one else was present, then turned to address the group.

"Meet back here at oh-seven-thirty," he said, simply. The group dispersed, and Strongman returned to his room to collect his belongings.

— § —

The debriefings had been mercifully short after the team returned to the Bunker at Fort Wadsworth. Once everything had been taken down for the record, Strongman was released to go back home.

From this point, Captain Freedom had two unenviable tasks: reporting to his superiors that they had been unable to secure the alien spacecraft, and worse yet, informing Brainpunch's next of kin about his death. The worst part of that was, because of the secrecy surrounding the team and its missions, all he would be able to tell them was that he had died in the line of duty. He couldn't say how, where, or why.

At least Strongman had been able to give that kind of closure to Nucleus' widow. She was just a few months pregnant with their first child when Nucleus was killed. She was raising their daughter alone, but Strongman had ensured that they were well taken care of, and was keeping watch over them, even if only from afar. The girl had just turned six, and as far as Strongman could tell, she seemed as normal as any other girl her age.

Strongman had never found that connection like Nucleus had. He'd had girlfriends, certainly, but none had ever proven to be serious enough for either of them to consider marriage. He was forty-two years old now, and he doubted that would change. There was too much that he could never share with a romantic partner, which proved ironic given that he was the first superhero to publicly reveal his identity. His years serving with Team Liberty, however, meant that there were some things that would have to remain a secret. Relationships were built on trust and openness, at least according to Nucleus, and how could he do that if he had to keep whole parts of his life secret from those closest to him?

Some of his former teammates on Team Liberty managed it, somehow. Even Samson had a family. Strongman didn't know how they managed to do it. He wasn't sure he would be able to do so.

He dropped his bag on the end of his bed. He resided in the master bedroom now. His parents had passed away years earlier, when he had been in Vietnam. They had been killed in a plane crash while en route to vacation in Europe, and he'd been granted leave to return to New York for their funeral. Their bodies had never been recovered after the plane crashed in the ocean, but the wreckage of the aircraft had been found and there was little doubt that no one aboard had survived. The caskets had been empty, but it at least gave him some small measure of closure.

The house was largely empty and incredibly quiet now, without his parents around. The staff were still there, of course, and there was always some level of activity, but nowhere near the levels it had been in years past. He began to remove the clasp holding his cape to the tunic of his costume, but paused once his fingers had found the buckle. The house was too quiet. His mind was just the opposite. He needed to get out, and he needed to do something.

He walked out onto the grounds in front of the house, exchanging greetings with the staff that maintained the house, prepared his meals, and kept everything running far better than he could ever hope to accomplish. Once outside, he leaped into the air, his strength propelling him almost as well as though he were able to fly. He soared over fields, forests, and buildings, making his way steadily toward Manhattan.

Once he arrived at the island borough, he found his way to the headquarters of the Minutemen, the team of superheroes that he and Nucleus had helped to form. The team's headquarters was located in a squat, otherwise nondescript three-story building just south of Thomas Jefferson Park, on the shoreline of the Harlem River, across from Randalls Island. The endowment he had provided for the team had been well invested, and it provided funding for the building and its upkeep, as well as the team's costumes and equipment.

He landed on the roof, and—passing the reinforced landing pad with the team's dedicated jump jet, which possessed vertical take-off and landing capabilities—he entered through the access door. He made his way downstairs to the team's meeting room on the third floor, which featured an enormous oval table with fifteen chairs spaced around it. The team's membership fluctuated over time, of course, but at the moment there were only ten members. The building was rarely empty, though, as the team maintained a watch rotation in case anything should happen that would require the team's mobilization.

Continuing down to the ground floor, Strongman passed through the large garage area that housed the team's ground vehicles. He entered a room located just off the garage, and inside he found two people sitting in front of a panel of radios and television monitors. They were listening to police and emergency bands, and watching for breaking news reports on both the major and local television networks. If something happened in New York that needed their intervention, the people on monitor duty would be the first to find out. The pair looked up at the newcomer and stood up quickly, smiles spreading across their faces.

"Strongman!" Phaser practically shouted as she embraced him in a hug. She was one of the team's newer recruits. A blonde woman in her early thirties, Cheryl Resorld discovered that she had the ability to phase her body through solid objects at will, and decided to use that ability to become a crime fighter.

"Glad to see you're back," her companion added. The dark-haired woman was the latest to take on the title of the Black Cobra. Renae Hornsby was the daughter of the third Black Cobra, Bob Hornsby. Bob had enlisted out of a sense of duty at the onset of the Vietnam War, and had sadly been killed in action during that conflict. Renae, now eighteen, had long known that her father was the Cobra Kid, and later the Black Cobra. After his death, she spent years honing her skills as both a fighter and a detective, and took up the mantle a few months earlier. "I trust your... *vacation* went well?"

"More or less," Strongman said, as Phaser finally began to release him from the hug. From the tone of her voice, it was clear that the newest Black Cobra didn't buy the cover story about his absence from New York. Given his own recent history with Team Liberty during the war, it probably didn't take a detective of her caliber to figure out that the government probably had something to do with his impromptu departure.

"We're all glad you're back," Phaser gushed. "It's been pretty quiet the last few days, but everyone feels better with you on the job."

Strongman smiled. It was good to be home.

About the Author

Jeffrey Harlan is an independent author of superhero fiction and the founder of Confluent Press, an independent publishing imprint that provides editorial and design services to self-published and independent authors.

In 2012, he began publishing *The Protectorate*, an independent comic book series about a team of teenaged superheroes in Las Vegas, before realizing that not only was drawing an ongoing comic book much more difficult than he'd expected, he also enjoyed writing the stories far more than he did drawing them. In 2021, inspired by other prose superhero novels he'd read, he self-published *Donner und Blitzkrieg*, a prequel to *The Protectorate* that focused on that world's first superheroes. He soon followed that up with three novellas, adapted from the four completed issues of *The Protectorate*. The novellas greatly expanded on the original comics and completed the storyline from the incomplete and unpublished fifth issue. In 2022, Jeffrey edited the novellas into a single volume, which he published as *Invasion*.

A military brat, Jeffrey moved frequently throughout his life. He's been a journalist, an airman, an educator, a security officer, and more. He's lived in three countries and seven states, and has traveled the world. A lifelong Trekkie, he has a deep love of science fiction and superheroes. He lives in Southern California's San Bernardino Mountains with his wife, Megan, their dog, Lucky, and their cats, Dusty and Snowball.